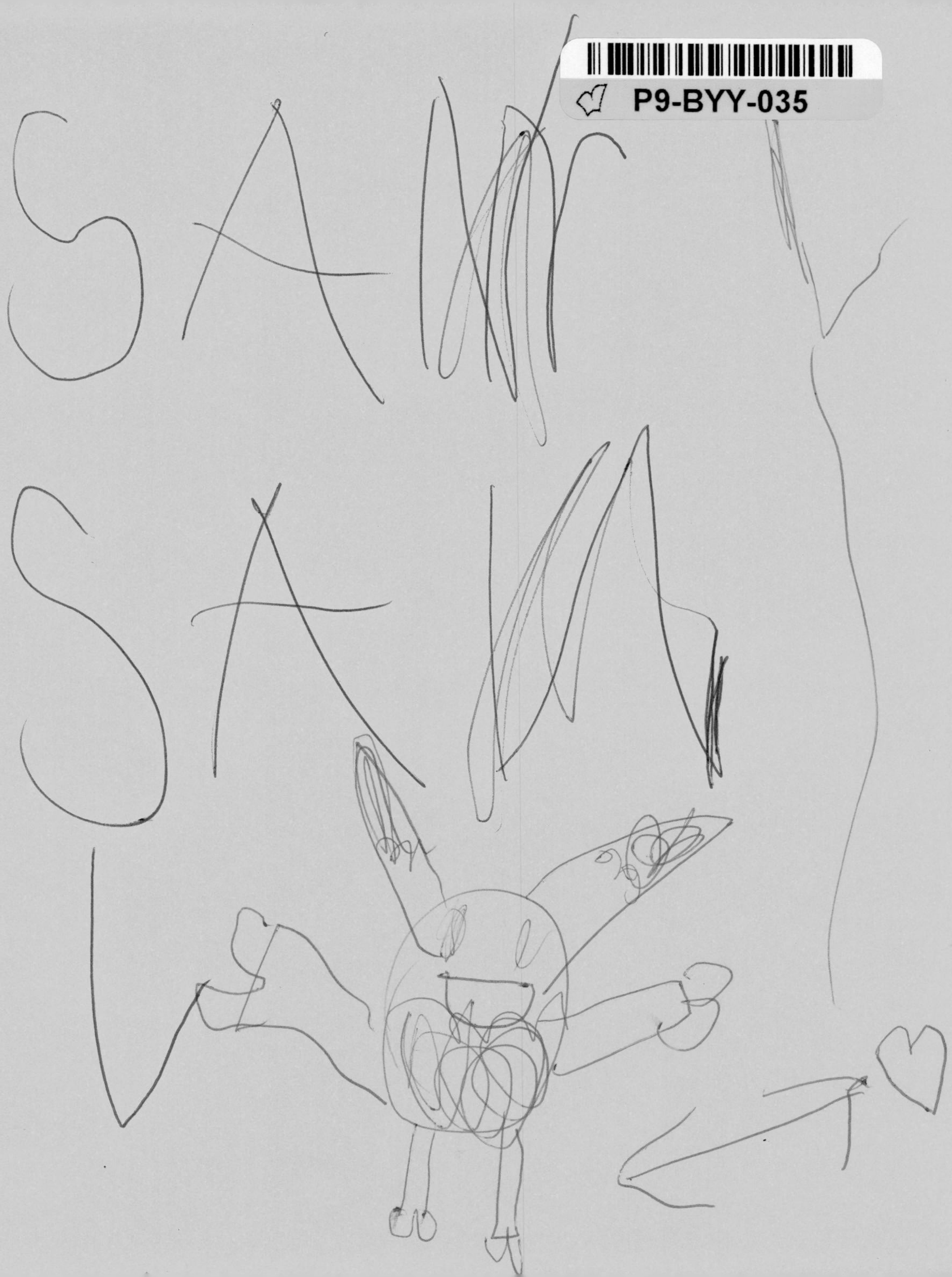
SAM
SAM

The
POKÉMON™
COOKBOOK
Easy & Fun Recipes

SUNFLORA

PIKACHU

PSYDUCK

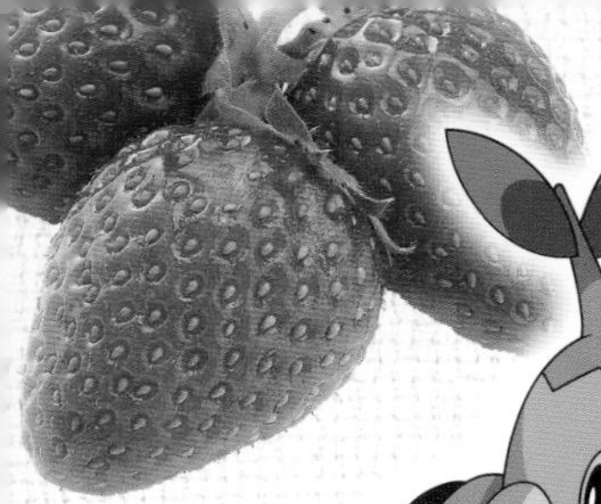

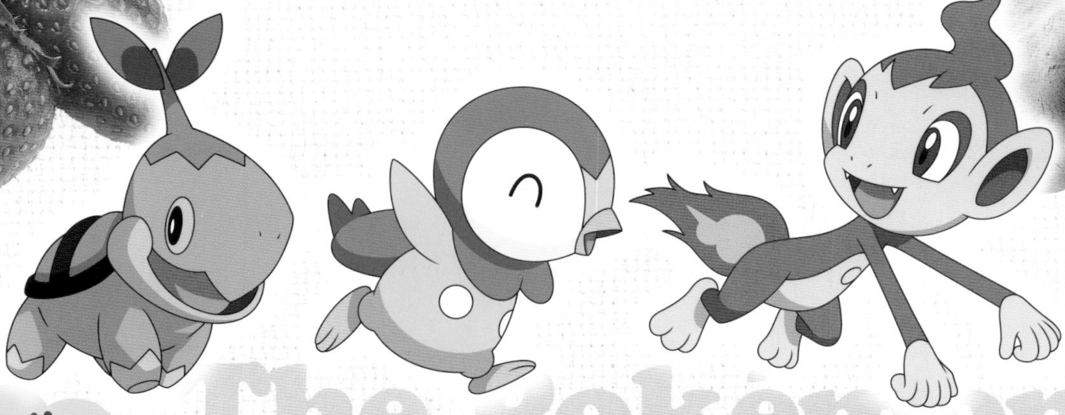

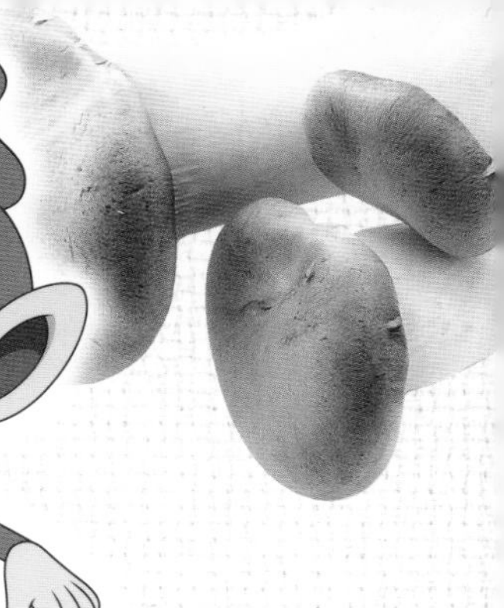

Let's make it!
Let's eat!

The Pokémon Cookbook

Let's do some Pokémon cooking!

For adults

This cookbook is based on the super-popular *Pokémon* characters.

The ingredients and recipes in this cookbook have been adjusted so that even children who have never cooked before can try these out. If you have children, please make the dishes together. As you cook, you can talk about favorite Pokémon. It's also a great opportunity to educate your kids about food. We hope this book can be used as a communication tool with your child.

Cooking will also teach them the following three eating habits.

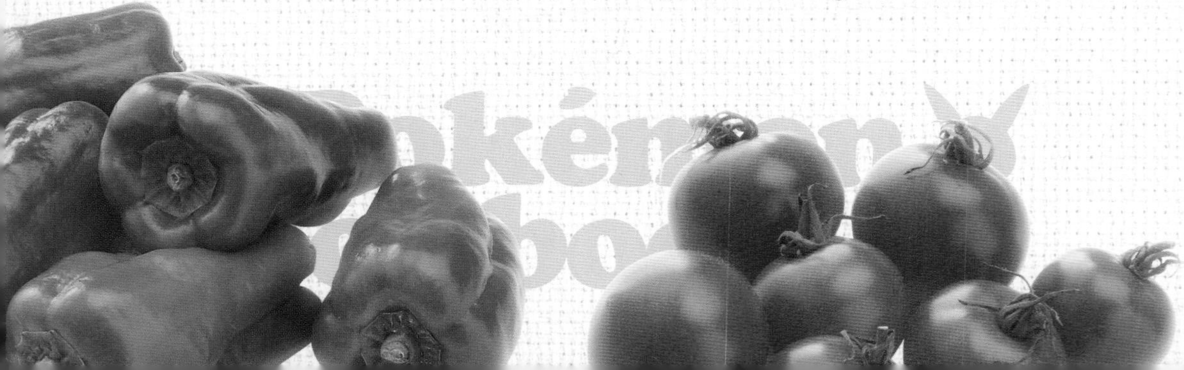

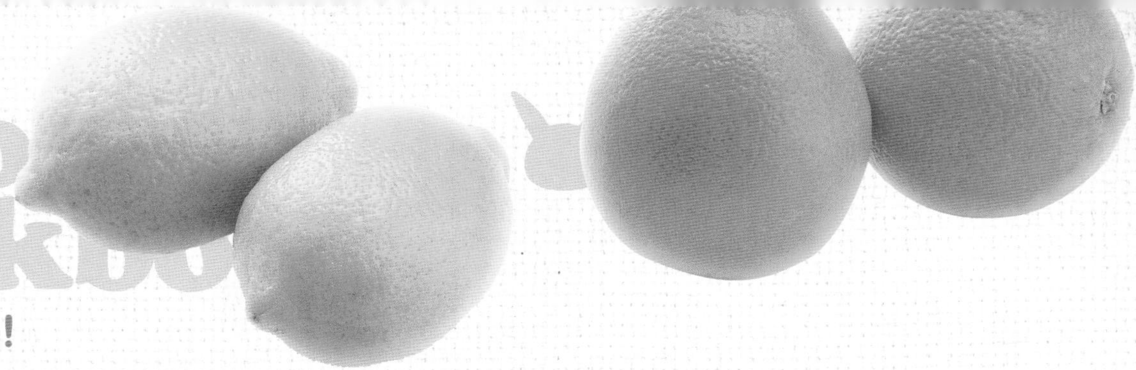

Enjoy eating!

Eating food is not just about getting the nutrients your body needs. You can also savor the different tastes and smells. You can chat with your family and friends as you sit down to a meal. And there are many things you can discover and learn through eating. Mealtimes are a really important part of your day. Be thankful for the food you eat every day, and have fun eating!

Eat a balanced meal!

There are nutrients in food that are necessary for your body. But nutrients are used in different ways inside your body. So be sure to eat a variety of foods to have a balanced meal. Don't knock something 'til you've tried it. Get all the nutrients you need by eating tasty dishes.

Eat three meals a day!

The nutrients you need to make energy to move or to build up a healthy body can't be achieved in one meal. Make sure to eat three square meals a day so that you can get a lot of nutrients. This is especially true for breakfast. If you start your day without eating, you won't have enough energy to last until lunch.
Eating a good breakfast is the best way to make sure you have a great day.

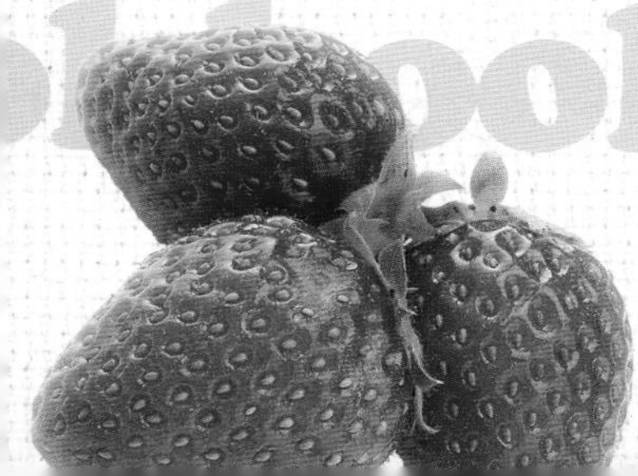

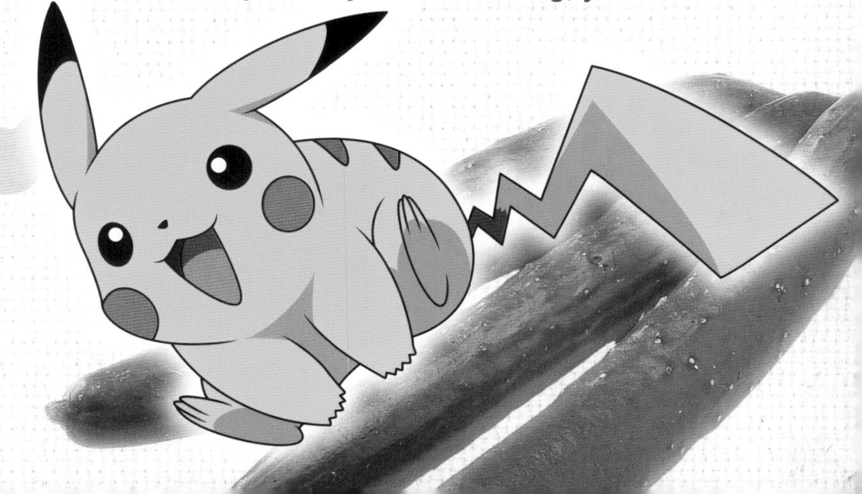

Contents

Part 1: Let's Have a Party!

Part 2: Exciting Lunchtime

Part 3: Summertime Fun

Part 4: Pokémon All-Stars

About the Tools Used in This Book

● Tablespoon & Teaspoon
A tablespoon is 15 milliliters. A teaspoon is 5 milliliters. Hold the tablespoon or teaspoon level when filling it. If you're filling it with a liquid, fill it all the way to the top. If you're filling it with a dry ingredient such as salt, fill it over the top (make a mound) and then use the back end of a butter knife to scrape the top part level.

● Measuring Cup
One cup is 237 milliliters. Rice measuring cups vary. Some are only 180 milliliters or ¾ cup, so please be careful.

● Scales
Place the scale on a level surface and make sure it's set to zero before using it.

Different Cutting Styles
Half-moon cut
Slice
Quarter cut
Julienne (cut into long strips)
Wedge cut
Mince (chop into tiny pieces)
Shred
Dice

● Bowls
If you mix the ingredients in a big bowl, they are less likely to spill out and you can mix vigorously. If you're putting it in the microwave, make sure to use a glass bowl or another microwave-safe type.

● Plastic Wrap
You may use this to cover bowls, to wrap ingredients to form a specific shape, or to cook something in the microwave.

● Microwave
A 500-watt microwave (low wattage) was used for the recipes in this book. The microwave you use may have a different wattage, so adjust your cooking time accordingly. The temperature of the food or plate and even the room temperature may cause your results to vary from what is pictured. You can shorten cooking times and check on the progress as you go along.

● Knives & Cutting Boards
If possible, use a knife that is designed for children's use. Make sure it can cut well. If using a wooden cutting board, wet it with water first. Use one side of the cutting board for raw meat/fish and the other for vegetables. After using, wash thoroughly and let dry.

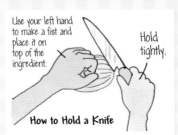

Use your left hand to make a fist and place it on top of the ingredient.
Hold tightly.
How to Hold a Knife

For more vibrant coloring, you can try to reduce cooking temperatures and cook dishes longer. Experiment with your Pokémon dishes.

Ask me anything about cooking!

Brock's Advice:

The **5** Points of Cooking!

There are five things I want you to do when cooking. Check them out!

Point 1

Prepare yourself!

Before you start cooking, prepare yourself. Put on an apron so your clothes don't get dirty. Tie up your hair with an elastic tie, pin it back with a hairpin, or wear a bandanna so your hair won't fall into the food. Keep your nails short, and wash your hands with soap.

Point 2

Gather your tools and ingredients before you start!

Oh no! It'll be bad if you realize you forgot something while you're cooking! So before you start, gather up all the ingredients, spices, and tools that you'll be using. Place them on the counter so that they're within easy reach.

Once you've prepared yourself, you'll be in the right mind-set to start!

You should have the plates ready too!

Point 3 Know the cooking order in your head!

Once you know what you're going to make, read the instructions carefully. You don't need to remember the exact measurements, but if you have an idea of the cooking order, everything will go smoothly. If there's something you don't understand in the instructions, ask an adult.

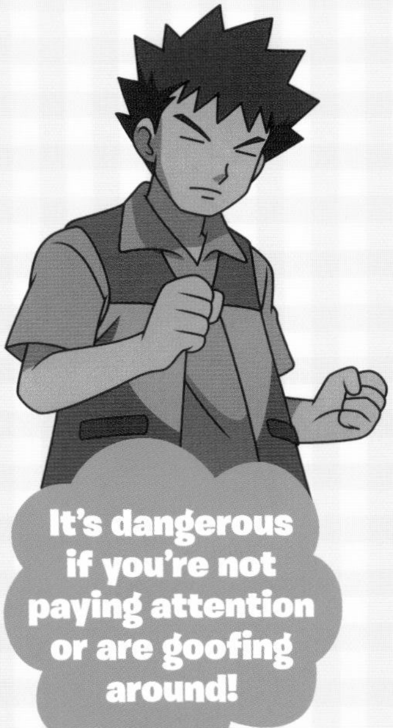
It's dangerous if you're not paying attention or are goofing around!

Don't forget these pointers!

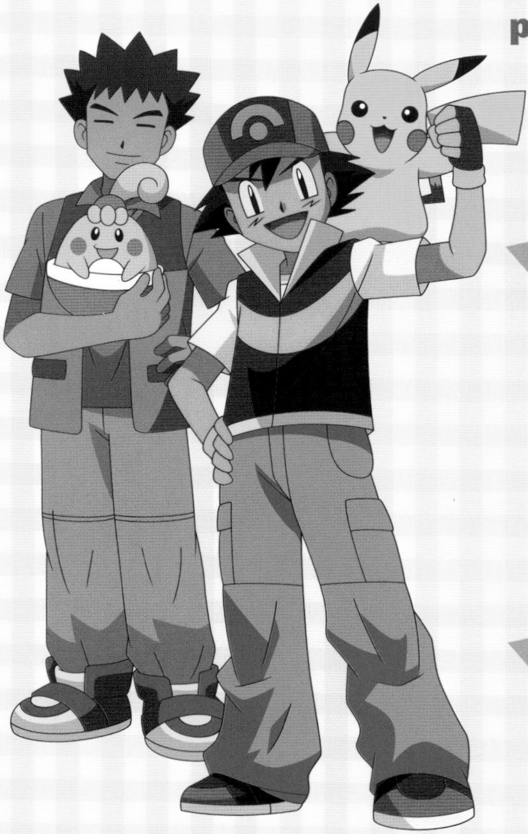

Point 4 Pay attention to your hands!

Knives are necessary cooking tools, but they can be dangerous when mishandled. When you have a knife in your hand, pay attention to what you're doing and be careful. Also, pay attention when you're using the stove top or hot water.

Point 5 Don't forget to clean up!

After cooking and then eating your delicious dishes, don't forget to clean up. Wash any tools or plates that you used and put them back where they belong. Wipe off any dirty tables or countertops. And lastly, throw out the trash. If you do this, you'll be perfect!

If you follow the rules, you can make delicious food!

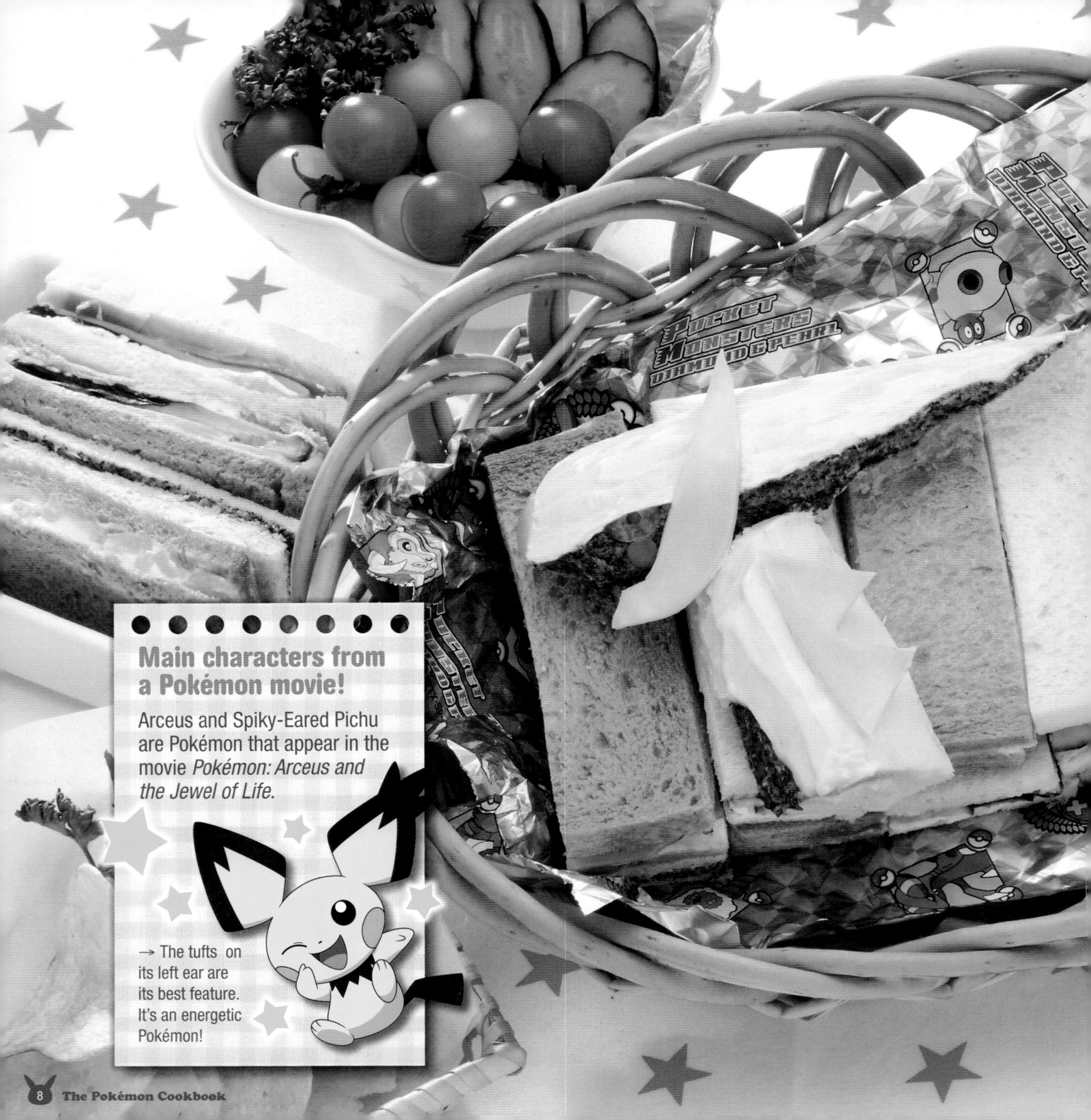
POCKET MONSTERS DIAMOND & PEARL

Main characters from a Pokémon movie!

Arceus and Spiky-Eared Pichu are Pokémon that appear in the movie *Pokémon: Arceus and the Jewel of Life*.

→ The tufts on its left ear are its best feature. It's an energetic Pokémon!

Lots of cream cheese!

Arceus Special Sandwich

Recipe on page 10

A fluffy cake you make with a steamer!

Spiky-Eared Pichu Egg Cake

Recipe on page 11

Let's Have a Party!

★ Let's Have a Party! ★ Let's Have a Party! ★ Let's Have a Party! ★ Let's Have a Party! ★

Let's have a party with Pokémon food. This'll be so much fun!

Arceus Special Sandwich

Page 8

We'll be making three different sandwiches using cream cheese. Make a fierce-looking Arceus!

Ingredients:

- 2 snack bread buns* (hot dog bun, split, may be substituted)
- 3½ ounces cream cheese
- 1 tablespoon honey
- 1 tablespoon black sesame seed paste
- 1 slice cheese
- 1–2 green peas
- 1 red chili pepper
- 1 slice lemon peel
- 1 teaspoon mayonnaise
- 6 slices sandwich bread
- 1 slice canned pineapple
- half stalk celery, approximately 4 inches
- 1 slice ham
- 1 small cucumber, approximately 4 inches, thinly sliced

**Snack bread is a sweet bread sold in Japan.*

Instructions: Makes 3 servings.

1. Take the cream cheese out of the refrigerator and bring it to room temperature to soften. Place it in a bowl and use a fork to soften it up.
2. Take half of the cream cheese (1¾ ounces) and mix it with the honey to create a white paste. Next, take 1 ounce of the cream cheese and mix it with the black sesame seed paste to create a black paste.
3. Cut the bun as shown in the illustration and spread the black and white paste on with a spoon. Make Arceus by placing the cheese slice, the lemon peel, the peas, and the chili pepper on top as shown in the illustration below.
4. Make the sandwich. Spread the remaining ¾ ounce of cream cheese on the bread, put the thinly sliced cucumber and ham on top, and then top it off with one more slice of bread that has mayonnaise spread on the underside of it.
5. Slice the pineapple finely and mix it with the remaining white paste. Spread the pineapple paste on a slice of bread and top it with another slice of bread.
6. Finely chop the celery and add it to the remaining black paste. Spread the mixture on a slice of bread and top it with another slice.
7. Cut the sandwiches in easy-to-eat sizes and place Arceus on top.

Mythical Pokémon
Arceus

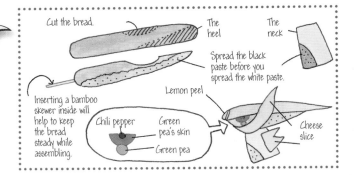

Cut the bread.
The heel
The neck
Spread the black paste before you spread the white paste.
Inserting a bamboo skewer inside will help to keep the bread steady while assembling.
Lemon peel
Chili pepper
Green pea's skin
Green pea
Cheese slice

Spiky-Eared Pichu Egg Cake

You can make different Pichu faces on top of the fluffy egg-colored cake!

Page 9

Ingredients:

- 2 eggs
- ¼ cup sugar
- 3½ ounces pancake mix
- 4 tablespoons milk
- 2 tablespoons vegetable oil
- 2 raisins
- 1 teaspoon strawberry jam
- 1 teaspoon cocoa powder
- 2–3 drops yellow food coloring

Instructions: Makes 1 cake / 4 servings.

1. Mix the eggs and sugar in a bowl.
2. Add the milk and vegetable oil to the mixture and mix well. Then add the pancake mix and blend until the batter is smooth. Add 2 to 3 drops yellow food coloring to batter.
3. Pour the batter into foil baking cups, leaving a little room at the top (fill about ⅘ full).
4. Place water in a steamer or double boiler. When steam starts to come out, place the foil cups inside. Place a cloth over the steamer and then place the lid on top. Steam on high heat for 15 minutes.
5. Once it's done, remove the lid to cool the cups.
6. Remove the cake from the baking cups and slice two layers off the bottom. Cut out the ears from bottom layers. Use the raisins, strawberry jam, and cocoa powder to make Pichu's face.

Pour batter until ⅘ full.
Be careful that the foil cups don't burn!
Steam at high heat.
Cut like this.
Make this the face.
Slice two pieces off the bottom (¼ inch each).
Cut a piece of paper in the shape of the ear and place it on top of the cake slice. Sprinkle cocoa powder on top to create the ears' dark edges.

Tiny Mouse Pokémon
Spiky-Eared Pichu

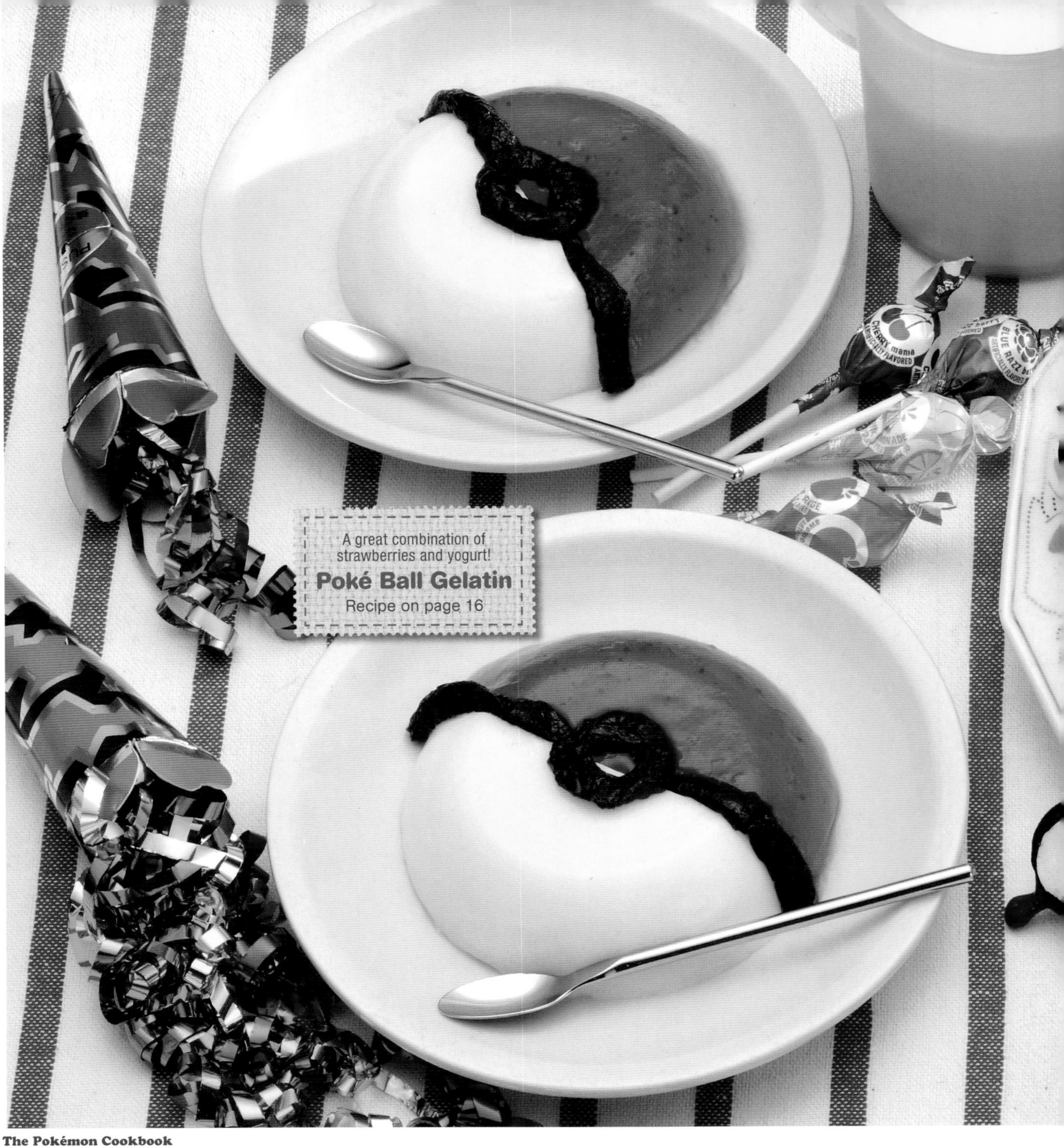

A great combination of strawberries and yogurt!

Poké Ball Gelatin

Recipe on page 16

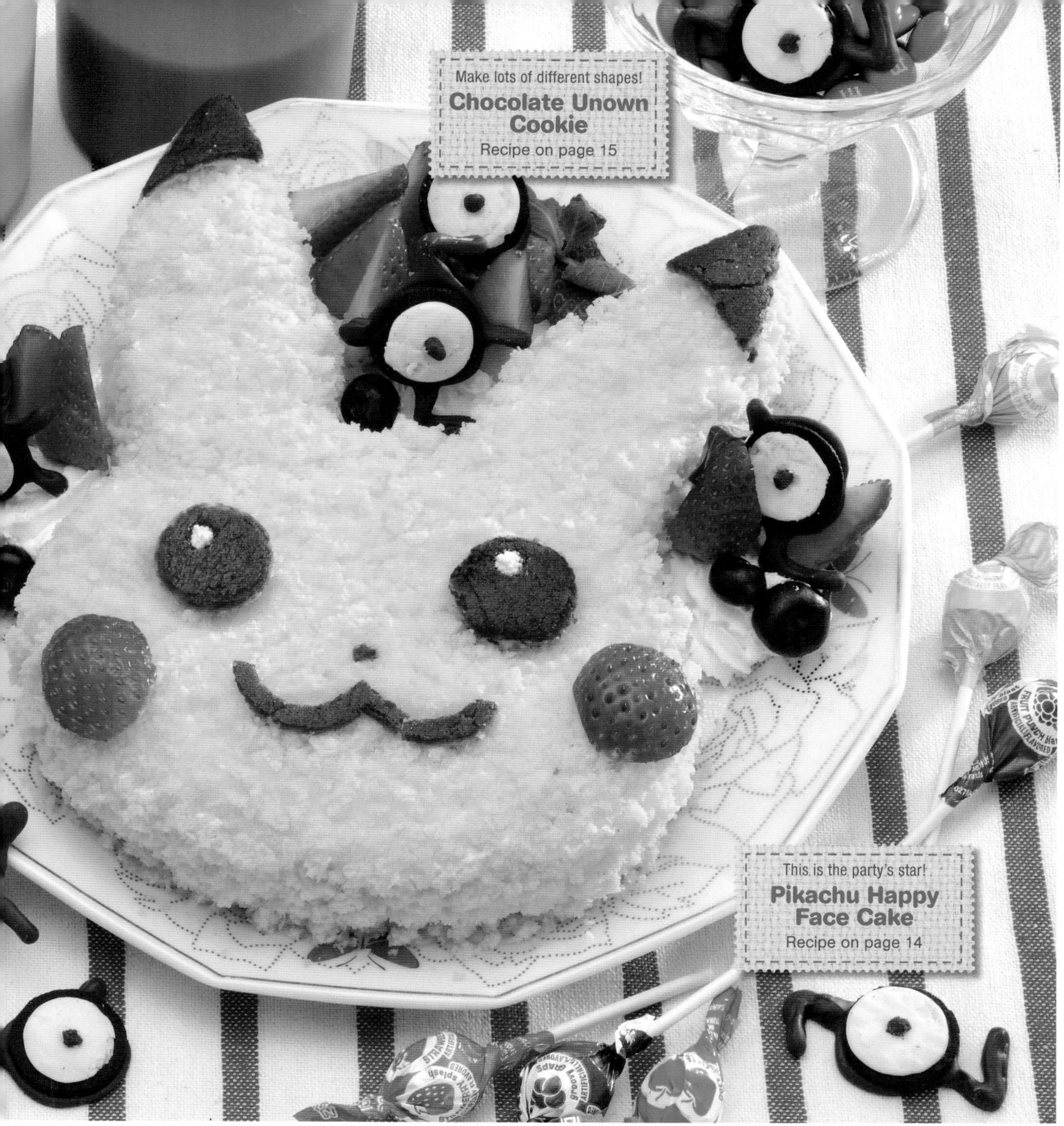

Make lots of different shapes!

Chocolate Unown Cookie

Recipe on page 15

This is the party's star!

Pikachu Happy Face Cake

Recipe on page 14

Pikachu Happy Face Cake

Page 13

A fluffy cake that looks like a stuffed animal. The secret to Pikachu's fluffiness is castella bits placed on top of the cream.

★ ★

Ingredients:

- 8 pieces store-bought castella* (lemon cake loaf or similar yellow cake may be substituted)
- ⅞ cup heavy whipping cream
- 8–10 strawberries
- 4 tablespoons sugar
- 2 teaspoons lemon juice
- 4 tablespoons water
- brown food coloring (optional—for use with lemon cake or other cake)

**Castella cake is readily available in Japan. It is usually a long brick shape that is cut up into slices. The cake has a brown crust on top and a crystallized-sugar layer on the bottom.*

Instructions: Makes 1 cake.

1. Wash the strawberries and remove the leaves. Slice them vertically in ¼-inch portions.
2. Mix the whipping cream with 2 tablespoons of sugar and whip until stiff.
3. Add 2 tablespoons of sugar to 4 tablespoons of water and microwave the mixture for 15 to 30 seconds to melt the sugar. When the liquid has cooled, add 2 teaspoons of lemon juice to create the syrup.
4. Place 6 pieces of castella as shown in the illustration and cut out Pikachu's face. Then slice each piece in half (thickness-wise).
5. Use a brush to spread the syrup on top of the bottom slice of castella. Then spread the whipped cream over that. Place the sliced strawberries on top and then cover with another layer of whipped cream.
6. Place the upper slice of the castella on top and brush it with syrup. Cover everything with a layer of whipped cream.
7. Separate the brown layer from the remaining castella, as well as from the leftover pieces that were cut. Place the castella into a bowl and use two forks to crumble the castella.
8. Spinkle the castella crumbs on the cake. Use the brown layers and the strawberries to create Pikachu's face.

Mouse Pokémon

Pikachu

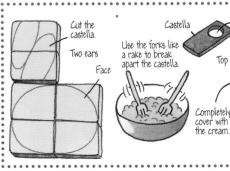

Cut the castella.
Two ears
Face
Castella
Use the forks like a rake to break apart the castella.
Use the brown parts to create the eyes and mouth. If you are using a different yellow cake, add a drop or two of brown food coloring (mix orange and blue food coloring together).
Top layer
Whipped cream
Strawberry
Bottom layer
Completely cover with the cream.
☆Be sure to assemble the cake on the plate you'll be using to serve it.

Chocolate Unown Cookie

Page 13

These are actually chocolate sandwich cookies!
It'll be easier if you have a sketch of Unown drawn out
before you start making the shapes with chocolate!

★ ★

Ingredients:

10 mini chocolate sandwich cookies

½ milk chocolate candy bar

Instructions: Makes 10 pieces.

1. Remove the top cookie from the chocolate sandwich cookie so that the cream filling is facing up.

2. Place the chocolate bar in a plastic bag and break it into pieces. Put hot water in a bowl and place the plastic bag in the bowl to melt the chocolate inside.

3. Spread some parchment paper, cut a corner of the plastic bag, and squeeze out the chocolate in the form of Unown.

4. While the chocolate is still warm, place the cookie on top.

5. Place a dot of chocolate in the middle of the cream center to create the eyeball.

Helpful Hint

If the melted chocolate gets any water in it, it won't harden properly. Make sure to wipe off all the moisture in your plastic bag after melting the chocolate.

Separate the cookies.

Use the chocolate like a pen to draw on top of the sketch.

Place the chocolate on top of the separated cookie while it's still warm.

Sketch (placed underneath the parchment paper)

Chocolate eyeballs

Symbol Pokémon
Unown

Poké Ball Gelatin

You'll need two bowls that are the same size. Use a bowl that has a rounded bottom.

Page 12

★ ★

Ingredients:

1 teaspoon gelatin

¼ cup strawberry jam

1 teaspoon lemon juice

½ cup plain yogurt

3 tablespoons sugar

2 prunes

⅓ cup + 4 tablespoons water

Instructions: Makes 2 servings.

1. Soak the gelatin in 2 tablespoons of water.

2. Make the red gelatin first. Strain the strawberry jam.

3. In a microwave-safe bowl, add the strawberry jam, lemon juice, 1 tablespoon of sugar, ⅓ cup water, and half of the gelatin.

4. Microwave for 30 seconds to 1 minute. Stir the mixture until the gelatin has melted.

5. Make the white gelatin next. In a microwave-safe bowl, add the plain yogurt, 2 tablespoons of sugar, 2 tablespoons of water, and the remaining half of the gelatin. Microwave for 30 seconds to 1 minute. Stir the mixture until the gelatin has melted.

6. Place each of the two gelatin mixes into two separate bowls of the same size. In an ice water bath, stir the gelatin until it's smooth.

7. Place the bowls in the refrigerator for 2 hours until firm.

8. Now to decorate! Place the bowls in some hot water for just a second to make it easier to remove the gelatin. Place the gelatin upside down on a plate.

9. Cut each gelatin mold in half. Place half of each colored gelatin together to create a ball. Cut the prune to make the center decoration.

Make sure that there's the same amount of gelatin in each bowl.

Cut each gelatin mold in half and place one of each color together.

Cut the prune with kitchen scissors.

Cut a hole out of the center to create a button.

Helpful Hint

When adding gelatin to warm ingredients, make sure that it's completely melted. If the gelatin hasn't melted, it won't harden properly.

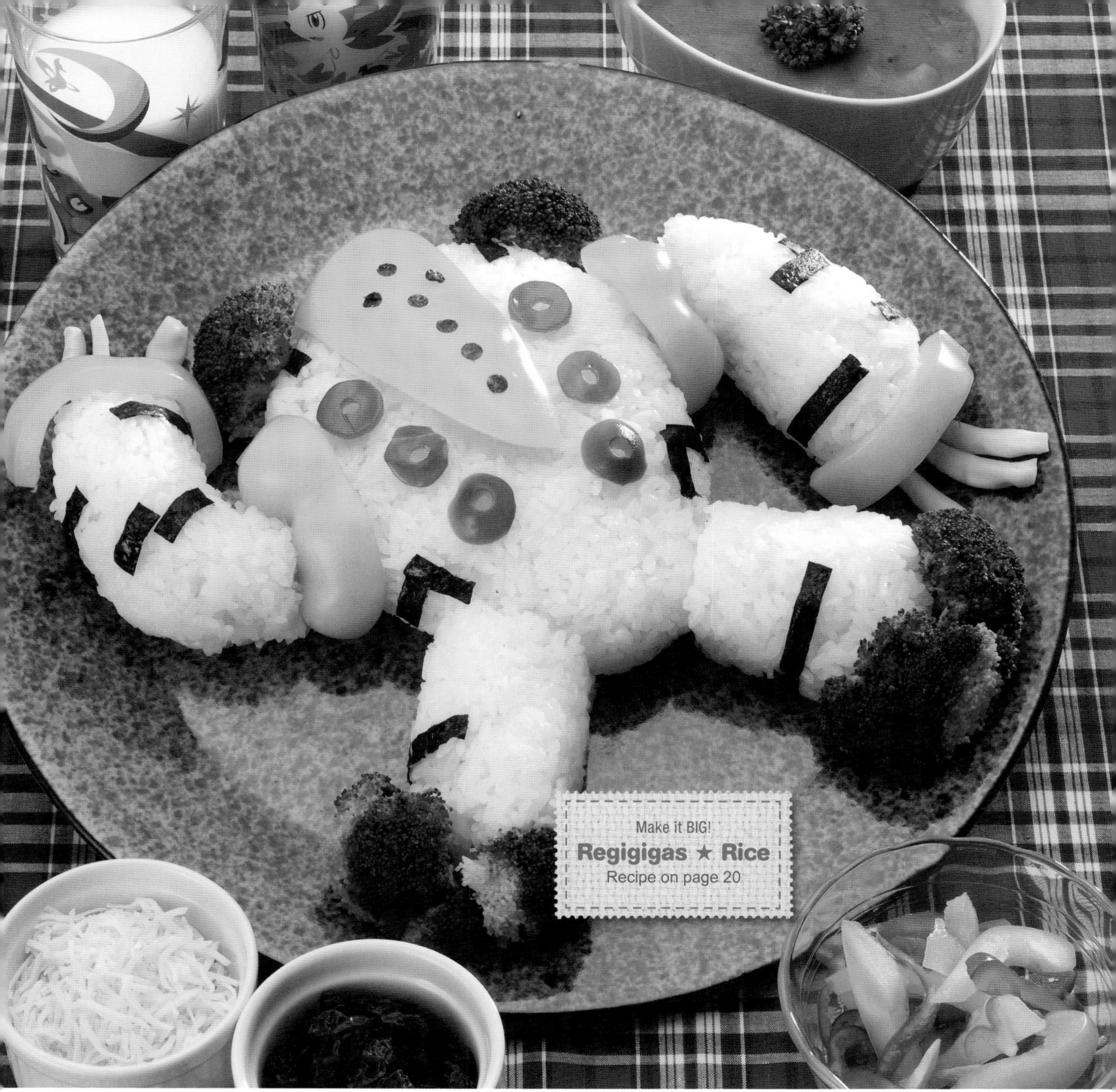
Make it BIG!
Regigigas ★ Rice
Recipe on page 20

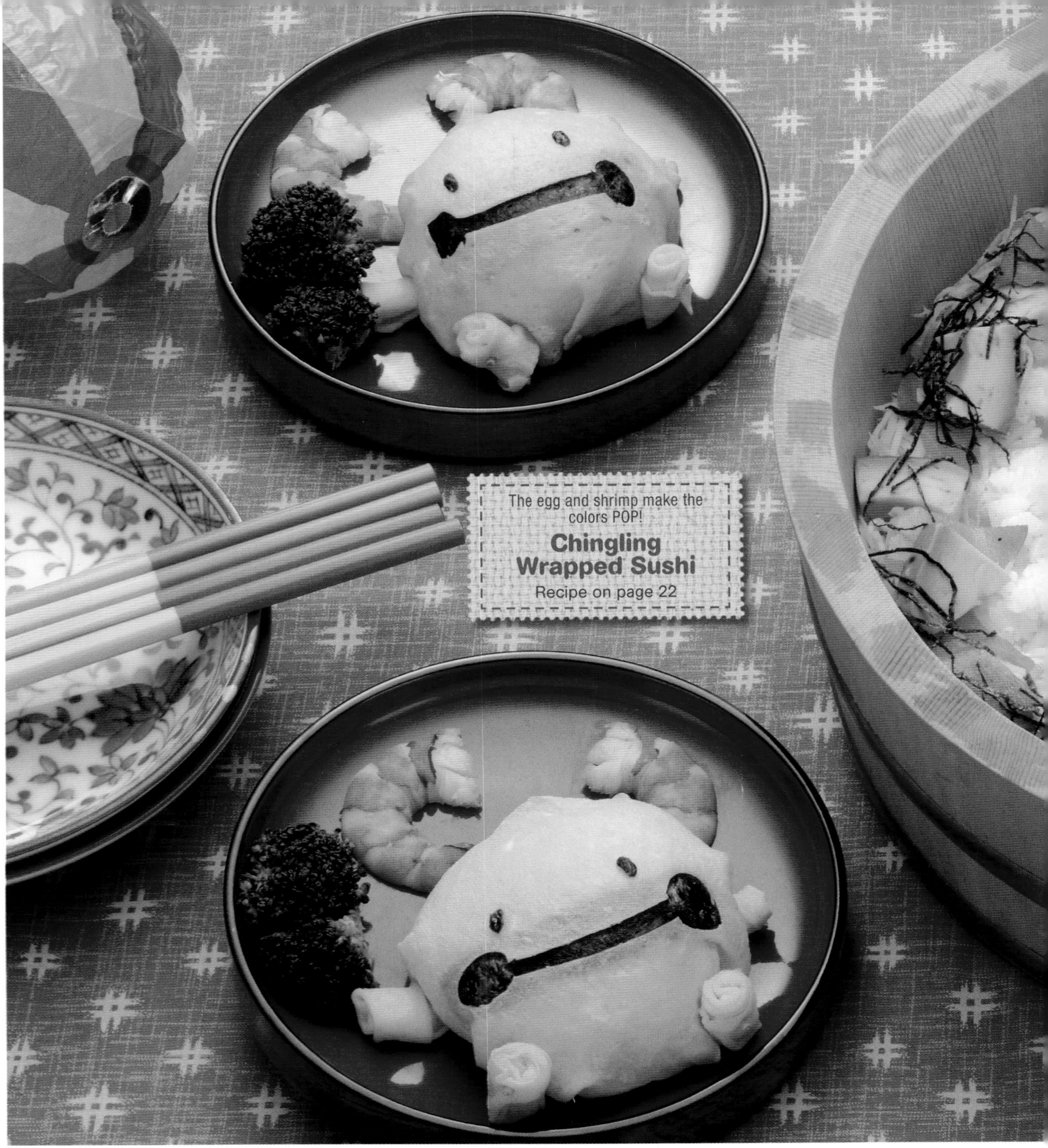

The egg and shrimp make the colors POP!

Chingling Wrapped Sushi

Recipe on page 22

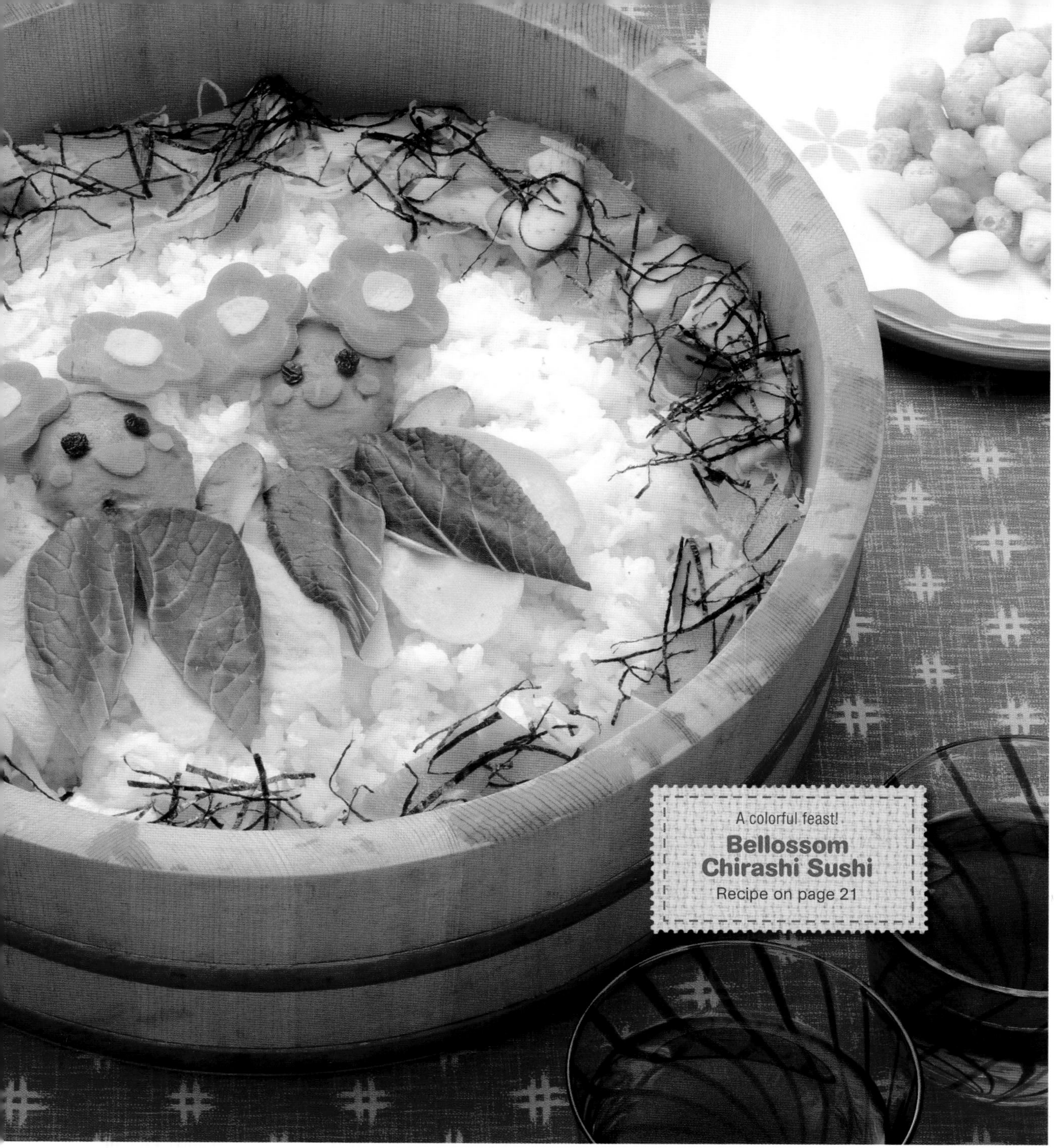

A colorful feast!

Bellossom Chirashi Sushi

Recipe on page 21

Regigigas ★ Rice

Rice is transformed into Regigigas. If you place it on a big plate, it'll really stand out!

Page 17

★ ★

Ingredients:

8 cups cooked rice (short-grain Japanese sticky rice recommended)

5–6 florets broccoli

1 yellow bell pepper

1 slice green bell pepper

1 slice red bell pepper

2 shimeji mushrooms

1 sheet nori (dried seaweed)

Instructions: Makes 3–4 servings.

1. Cut the broccoli into smaller pieces. Boil them in hot water approximately 3 to 5 minutes until cooked and set aside to cool.

2. Separate the individual shimeji mushrooms and microwave them for 30 seconds. Once cooled, separate the caps from the stems.

3. Place plastic wrap inside a large bowl and put half of the cooked rice on top. Shape the rice lightly. Take the wrapped rice out of the bowl and put it on a plate. Form the rice into the body shape of Regigigas.

4. Take the remaining rice and wrap it in plastic wrap. Shape it into a long, skinny form for the arms and legs.

5. Cut the yellow bell peppers as shown in the illustration and use it for the face, shoulders, and wrists.

6. Use the broccoli, the green bell pepper, the red bell pepper, the cap and stems of the shimeji mushrooms, and the nori to create Regigigas as shown in the illustration.

Colossal Pokémon

Regigigas

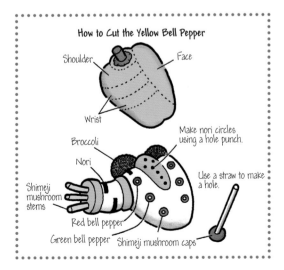

How to Cut the Yellow Bell Pepper

Shoulder

Face

Wrist

Make nori circles using a hole punch.

Broccoli

Nori

Use a straw to make a hole.

Shimeji mushroom stems

Red bell pepper

Green bell pepper

Shimeji mushroom caps

Bellossom Chirashi Sushi

The Bellossom cheerfully dance on top of the chirashi sushi! You can make the egg crepe part easily in the microwave.

★   ★

Ingredients:

1 pack smoked salmon

2 eggs

2 teaspoons sugar

2 teaspoons vegetable oil

pinch of salt

2 teaspoons cornstarch

2 teaspoons water

1 avocado

sprinkle of lemon juice

4 1-inch carrot slices

4 raisins

5–6 bok choy leaves

4 cups cooked rice

sushi rice seasoning*

handful of nori strips (dried seaweed)

*Sushi rice seasoning is a powder that you mix into hot rice that turns it into sushi rice easily. You can find this at Japanese grocery stores. To make sushi rice the old-fashioned way, you need to combine rice vinegar, sugar, and salt and then mix it into rice. See Helpful Hint on page 48.

Instructions: Makes 3–4 servings.

1. Whisk the eggs in a bowl. Use a metal sieve to strain the eggs. Mix 2 teaspoons of cornstarch with 2 teaspoons of water and set aside. Mix 2 teaspoons of sugar, 2 teaspoons of vegetable oil, and a pinch of salt. Add the cornstarch mixture and mix.

2. Wrap a large plate with plastic wrap and spread out the egg mixture in a 4-inch circle. Microwave for 30 seconds to 1 minute. Once the egg mixture has hardened, remove it from the microwave and peel it off the plastic wrap. Cut the portion to be used for Bellossom and slice up the remaining egg into thin strips.

3. Cut the avocado as shown in the illustration. Make the faces using raisins and carrots and create the hands using avocado. Cut the remaining avocado into two bite-sized portions and sprinkle with lemon juice to help retain the color.

4. Add a little water to the carrots, and microwave for 1 minute.

5. Add the sushi rice seasoning to the cooked rice to make sushi rice. Place in a serving bowl. Make the Bellossom using the avocado, carrots, egg, and bok choy on top of the sushi rice as shown in the illustration.

6. Along your serving bowl's edges, top the sushi rice with smoked salmon, avocado, thin egg strips, and nori strips.

Flower Pokémon

Bellossom

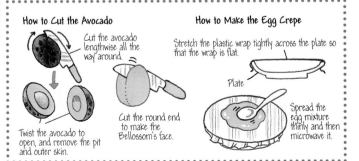

How to Cut the Avocado

Cut the avocado lengthwise all the way around.

Twist the avocado to open, and remove the pit and outer skin.

Cut the round end to make the Bellossom's face.

How to Make the Egg Crepe

Stretch the plastic wrap tightly across the plate so that the wrap is flat.

Plate

Spread the egg mixture thinly and then microwave it.

Chingling Wrapped Sushi

If you use a frying pan, you can make a bigger and better-looking egg crepe than with a microwave. Give it a try!

Page 18

Ingredients:

- 1 egg
- ¾ cup cooked rice (short-grain Japanese sticky rice recommended)
- sushi rice seasoning*
- 2 pieces shrimp in shell
- ½ sheet nori (dried seaweed)
- pinch of salt
- 1 teaspoon cornstarch
- 1 teaspoon + 3 cups water
- 1 teaspoon vegetable oil

Available at Japanese grocery stores, or see Helpful Hint on page 48.

Instructions: Makes 2 servings.

1. Whisk the egg in a bowl and strain it with a metal sieve. Add a pinch of salt and 1 teaspoon of cornstarch that has been mixed with 1 teaspoon of water.
2. On low heat, add 1 teaspoon of vegetable oil to the frying pan and spread it evenly using a paper towel.
3. Take ⅓ of the egg mix and add it to the frying pan. Quickly spread the mixture so that it covers the bottom of the pan.
4. When the edges of the egg separate from the pan, flip the crepe over and fry the other side. Remove when done. Repeat two more times.
5. Bring 3 cups of water to a boil. If desired, add a pinch of salt to the water, and then boil the shrimp with their shells still on for 2 minutes. Remove shrimp from the water and set aside to cool. Once the shrimp have cooled down, remove the shells and cut them in half lengthwise. If necessary, devein the shrimp. Snip off the bottom ends of the shrimp.
6. Add the sushi rice seasoning to the cooked rice to make sushi rice. Split the rice in half and form it into balls.
7. Place the rice on a plate and put a piece of nori on top to make Chingling's mouth as shown in the illustration. Wrap the egg crepe over the rice. Wrap the whole ball with plastic wrap and set aside. Repeat.
8. Cut the remaining egg crepe into ⅓-inch strips. Roll up each strip to create the hands and feet.
9. Remove the plastic wrap from the rice balls and cut out the mouth portion. Place the shrimp and rolled-up egg strips to create Chingling.

Helpful Hint

When making the egg crepe, use a clean frying pan that doesn't have any burnt bits on it. You'll have an easier time with a nonstick frying pan.

Bell Pokémon
Chingling

Place the nori on top of the ball of rice.
Put it just below the center.
Wrap the egg crepe around the rice and then wrap it in plastic wrap.
Use small ovals of nori for eyes.
Cut out a circle.
Cut out the mouth and open slightly.

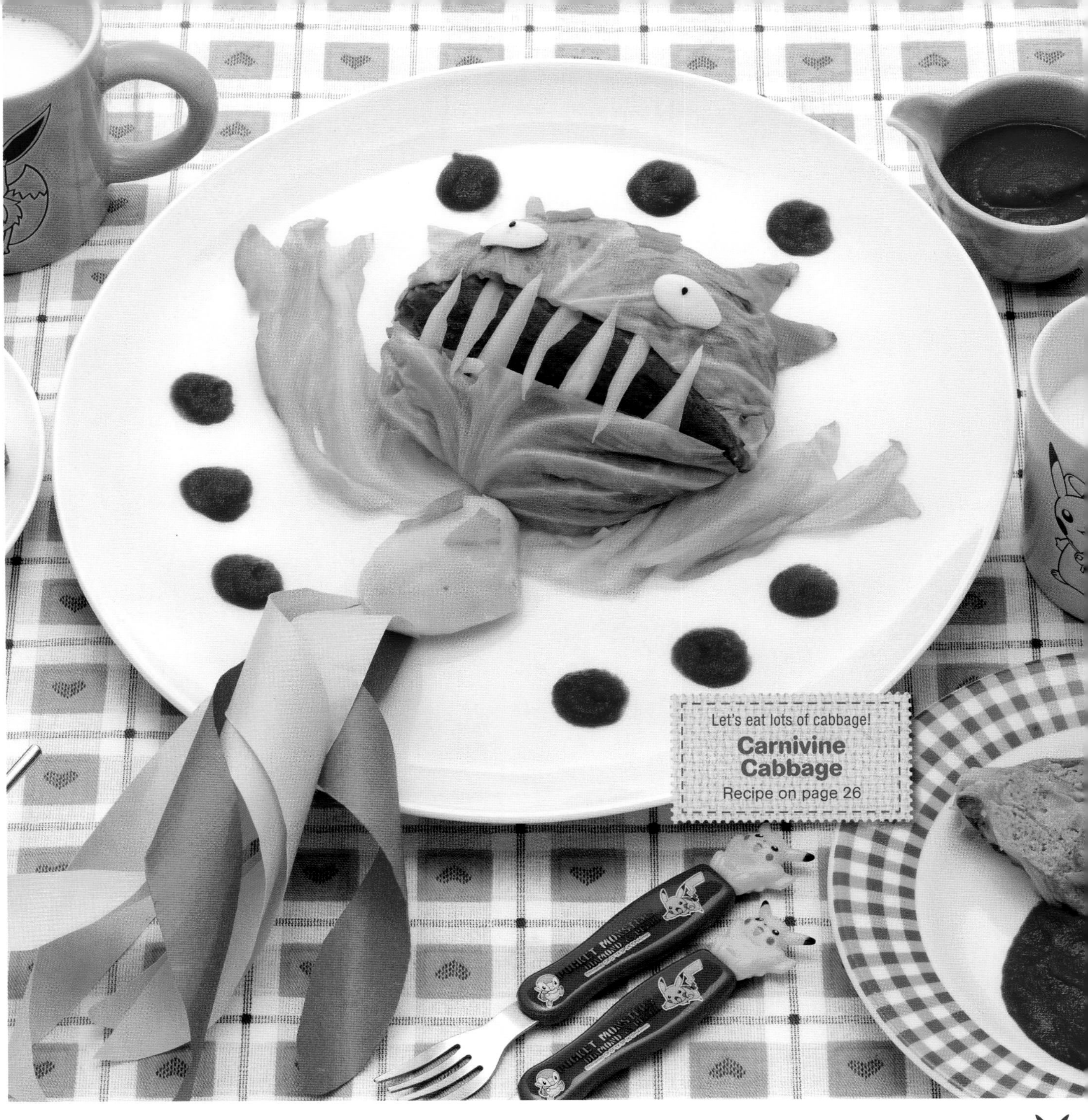

Let's eat lots of cabbage!

Carnivine Cabbage

Recipe on page 26

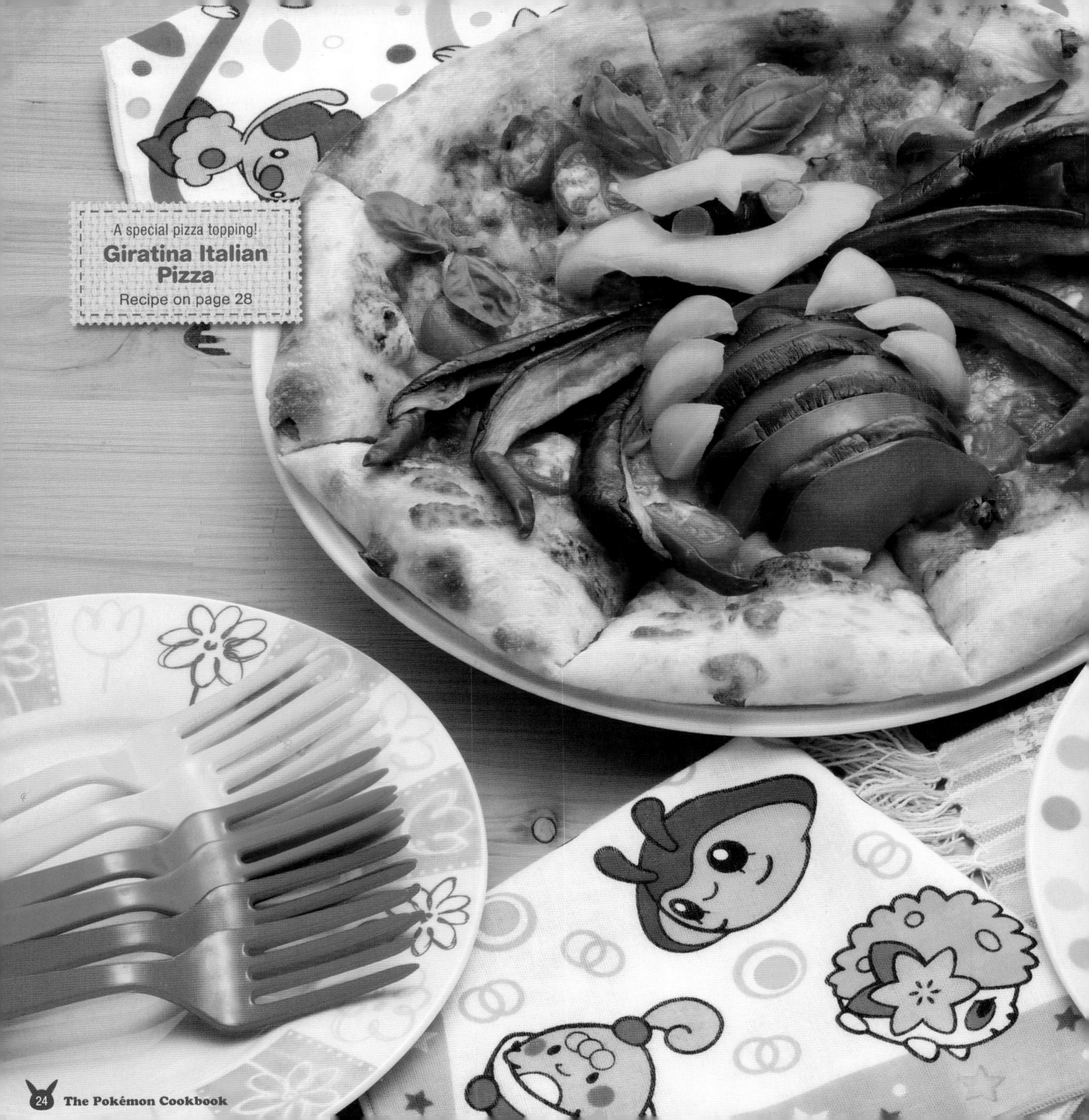

A special pizza topping!

Giratina Italian Pizza

Recipe on page 28

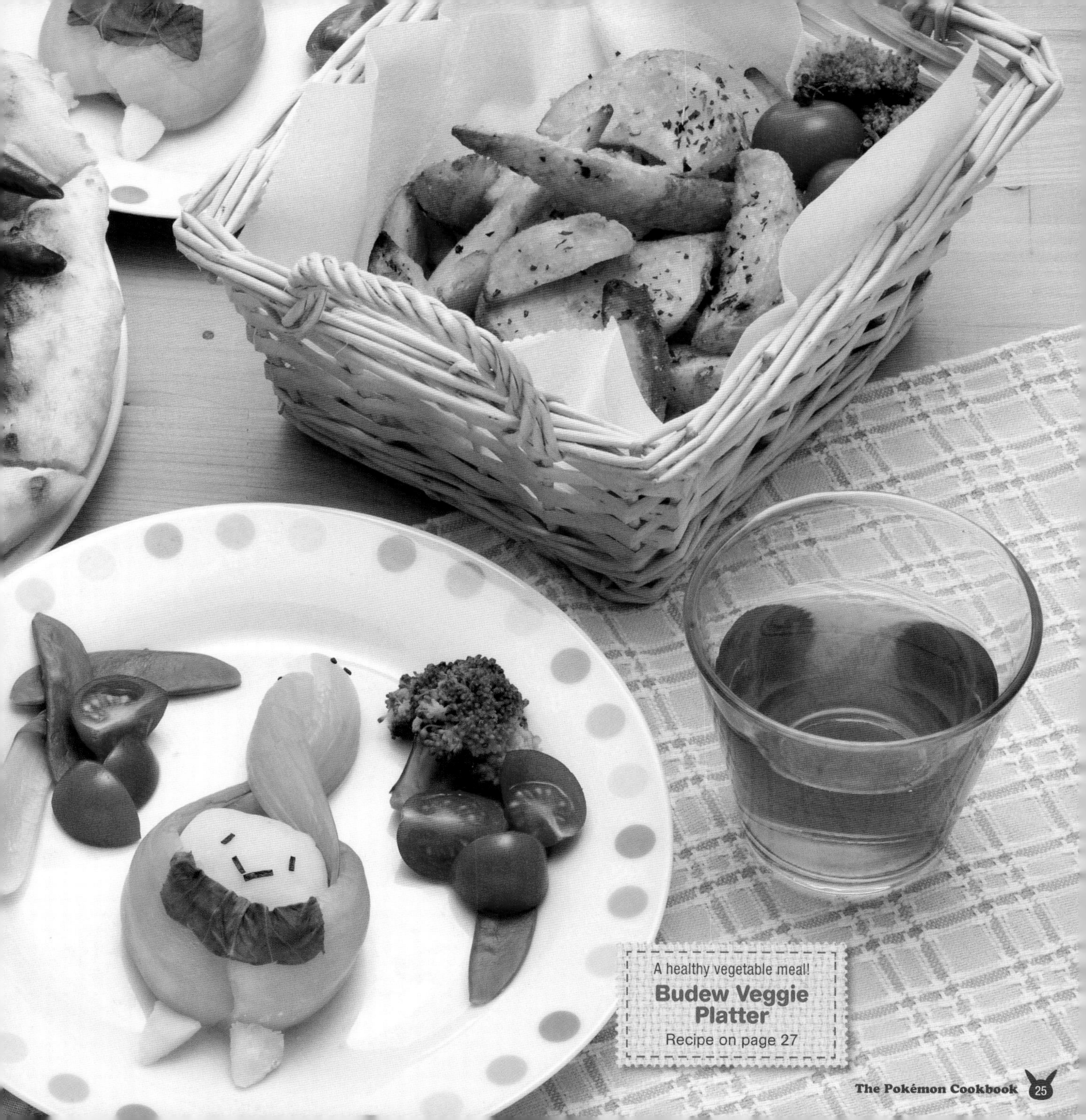

A healthy vegetable meal!

Budew Veggie Platter

Recipe on page 27

Carnivine Cabbage

Let's eat tasty cabbage that's sweet and soft. You can use a ribbon for its feet.

Page 23

★ ★

Ingredients:

7–8 leaves cabbage

½ pound ground-meat filling (recipe on page 27)

1 medium white potato

1 hard-boiled egg or quail egg

2 black sesame seeds

cornstarch to coat cabbage leaves

Instructions: Makes 5–6 servings.

1. Wash the cabbage leaves, place them in a plastic bag, and microwave them for 2 minutes.

2. Once the cabbage is cool to the touch, remove it from the bag and cut off the hard stems. Set stems aside.

3. In a microwave-safe bowl, spread out a cabbage leaf. Sprinkle some cornstarch on the leaf and then layer ⅓ of the ground meat so that it's flat.

4. Place another cabbage leaf on top of the ground meat, sprinkle some cornstarch, and layer ⅓ of the ground meat.

5. Repeat so you have three layers, and then place one cabbage leaf on top. Cover the bowl in plastic wrap and microwave for 8 minutes. Let sit for 5 minutes.

6. Remove the plastic wrap and put a plate over the top of the bowl. Tilt the bowl to drain any liquids. Flip the bowl over and remove it from the plate.

7. Cut the cabbage as shown in the illustration to make Carnivine's mouth. Add the cabbage bits to create its fangs.

8. Wrap the potato in a paper towel and microwave it for 3 to 5 minutes until fully cooked but still firm. Remove the potato skin and cut it in half. Use the potato and egg to create Carnivine as shown in the illustration.

Bug Catcher Pokémon

Carnivine

Cut off the cabbage stem at the bottom. The stem will be used for Carnivine's fangs, so don't throw it away!

Cabbage   Meat

Make three layers of meat and cabbage.

Remove this portion to make its mouth.

Cut the cabbage with scissors to make the hands.

Cut the round ends of the egg to make the eyes, and place a black sesame seed in the center of each.

Potato

Use a ribbon to make the legs.

Budew Veggie Platter

Page 25

This uses the same ground-meat filling as the Carnivine Cabbage on page 26. Be sure to eat the veggie decorations too!

★ ★ ★ ★ ★ ★ ★ ★ ★ ★ ★ ★ ★ ★ ★ ★ ★ ★ ★ ★

Ingredients:

2 bok choy

1 potato

3½ ounces ground-meat filling (see recipe below)

¼ sheet nori (dried seaweed)

3–4 black sesame seeds or 2 nori strips

cherry tomatoes (for decoration)

snow peas (for decoration)

broccoli (for decoration)

Instructions: Makes 3 servings.

1. Pull apart the leaves of the bok choy and place them in a plastic bag. Microwave for 2 minutes.

2. Wrap the potato in a paper towel and microwave for 3 minutes. Peel the skin off.

3. Wet your hands and make three meatballs with the ground-meat filling. Place them on a plate and flatten the tops.

4. Loosely place plastic wrap over the meatballs and microwave for 3 minutes.

5. Cut the round end of the potato and place it on top of a meatball to make the face. Cut the bok choy as shown in the illustration and wrap the potato to make a Budew.

6. Decorate the plate with your favorite vegetables.

★Ground-Meat Filling

Ingredients: Makes 1 Carnivine or 6–7 Budew meatballs.

7 ounces ground pork or beef

1 egg

½ carrot, grated

½ teaspoon grated ginger

2 tablespoons green onions, chopped

½ teaspoon salt

1 teaspoon soy sauce

Instructions:

1. Place the ground meat and egg in a bowl and grind the carrot into it. Mix together.

2. Mix in the grated ginger and the green onions, and then mix in the salt and soy sauce.

Bud Pokémon

Budew

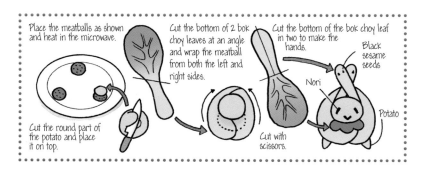

Place the meatballs as shown and heat in the microwave.

Cut the round part of the potato and place it on top.

Cut the bottom of 2 bok choy leaves at an angle and wrap the meatball from both the left and right sides.

Cut with scissors.

Cut the bottom of the bok choy leaf in two to make the hands.

Black sesame seeds

Nori

Potato

Giratina Italian Pizza  Page 24

We made an original Giratina pizza from eggplants and tomatoes—staples of Italian cuisine. Place them on top of cooked pizza dough and you're all set!

★ ►

Ingredients:

2 medium eggplants

½ tomato

2 tablespoons olive oil

1 yellow bell pepper

6 red chili peppers

store-bought pizza dough

Instructions: Makes 1 serving.

1. Cut the tomato in a half-moon shape ⅓ inch wide. Cut one of the eggplants width-wise into ⅓-inch-wide rounds. Cut the other eggplant lengthwise into 6 pieces.

2. Put the olive oil in a frying pan and cook the eggplant over medium heat. Remove from the pan.

3. Alternate the round eggplant slices and the tomato slices on top of a cooked, store-bought pizza dough to make Giratina's body.

4. Cut the yellow bell pepper to create the face.

5. Pierce the chili peppers with a toothpick and insert them into the ends of the lengthwise eggplant.

Renegade Pokémon

Giratina

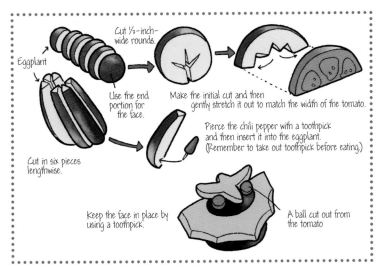

Eggplant

Cut ⅓-inch-wide rounds.

Use the end portion for the face.

Make the initial cut and then gently stretch it out to match the width of the tomato.

Cut in six pieces lengthwise.

Pierce the chili pepper with a toothpick and then insert it into the eggplant. (Remember to take out toothpick before eating.)

Keep the face in place by using a toothpick.

A ball cut out from the tomato

A Catalog of Handy Ingredients

Here are some handy ingredients you'll use for your Pokémon recipes. Some items can be found in Asian food stores or the Asian food aisle of grocery stores.

Mixed Beans & Mixed Vegetables

Mixed beans are a combination of three different beans that have already been boiled. They're used as ingredients for salad. They come either canned or in a plastic bag. You can also easily make mixed beans by buying the individual ingredients and mixing them together.

Mixed vegetables are a mix of corn, carrots, and green peas. They're really colorful, so they're great for added decoration.

→ The mixed beans—kidney beans (top), green peas (bottom left), and chickpeas (bottom right).

Dried Fruits & Jam

Dried fruits like raisins and prunes are perfect for making small parts. Just cut them using kitchen scissors. Bright-red strawberry jam and purple, blueberry, or grape jam will make your desserts pop with color.

→ (clockwise from the top) Raisins, maraschino cherries, prunes, and cranberries.

Sliced Cheese, Kamaboko (fish cake) & Nori (dried seaweed)

These can be cut into many different shapes and they're easy to use, so they are super handy for making Pokémon parts. Cheese slices are good for Western dishes. Be careful if you use them on hot foods since they'll melt. For Japanese dishes, kamaboko and nori are useful.

Chocolate Candy, Jelly Beans & Amanatto (sugared beans)

Colorful jelly beans and different chocolate candies are useful when making Pokémon desserts. They can even serve as toppings. Amanatto is soft, is easy to use, and has a simple flavor, so you can use it in a variety of ways.

↑ Amanatto variety (clockwise from the top): green peas, red kidney beans, white beans, and azuki red beans. Use them according to their colors and shapes.

↑ Jelly beans (left) and candy-coated chocolates (right). The color of the candy-coated chocolates will dissolve if they get wet, so add them last.

EASY ★ OMELET

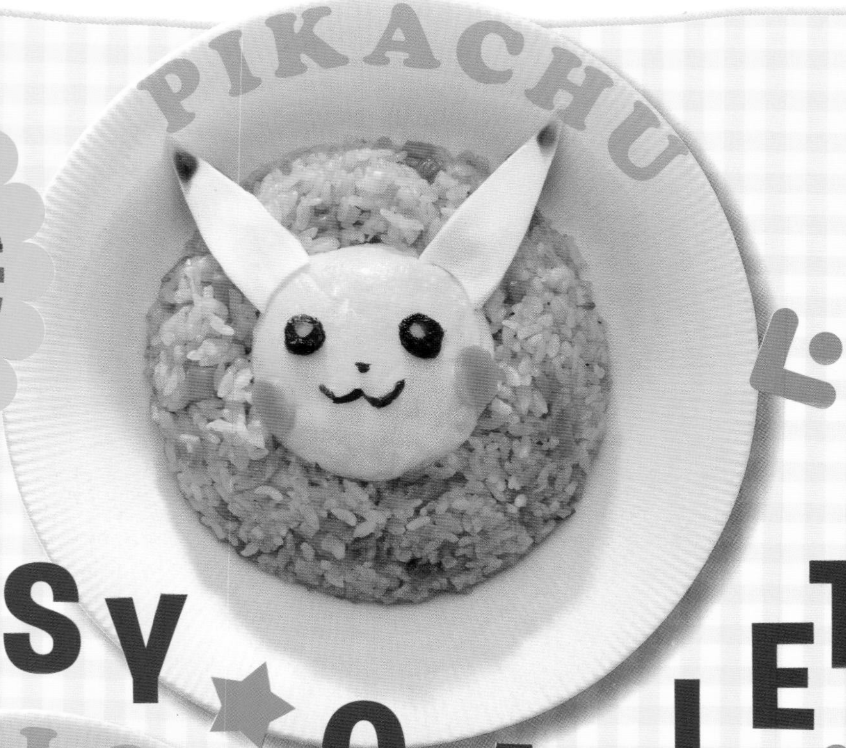
PIKACHU

Pikachu

You can change its facial expressions just by altering the placement of its ears.

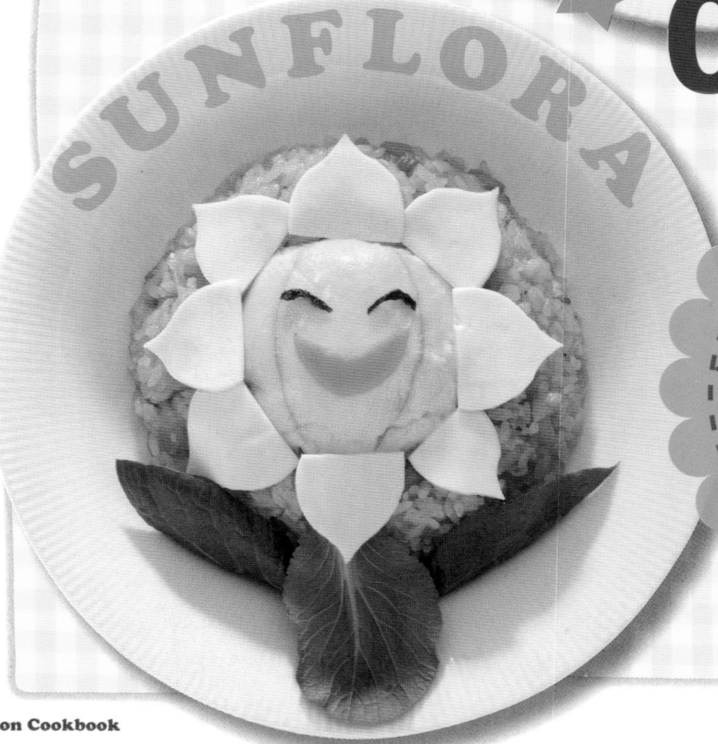
SUNFLORA

Sunflora

Its smile will brighten up any table!

Exciting Lunchtime

Have a fun lunch with your favorite Pokémon!

Exciting Lunchtime ★ Exciting Lunchtime ★

RICE TRIO

Make three different Pokémon using one omelet recipe!

Basic Omelet Rice

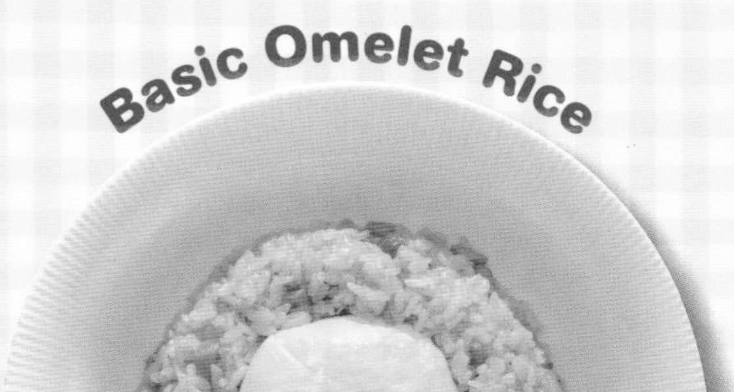

PSYDUCK

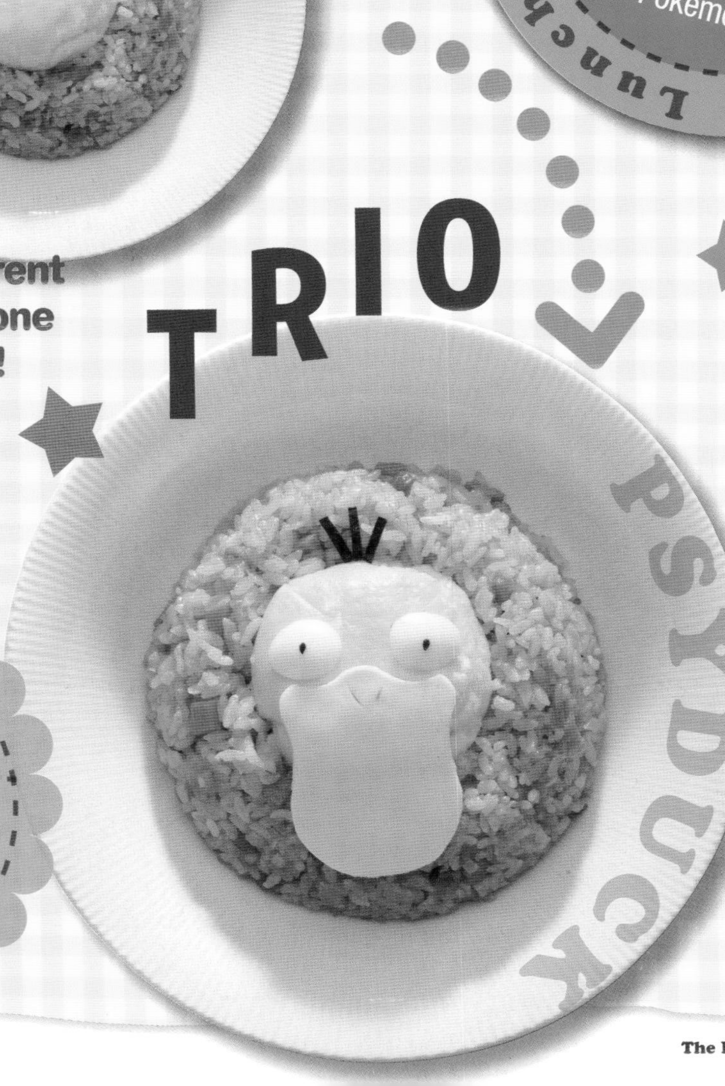

Psyduck

Its best features are its big bill and the three little hairs on the top of its head. ♪

Easy Omelet Rice Trio

First, let's make the basic omelet rice. You just need to place a round omelet on top of some ketchup rice!

Pages 30–31

Duck Pokémon
Psyduck

Sun Pokémon
Sunflora

★ ★

Ingredients:

⅔ cup cooked rice (short-grain Japanese sticky rice recommended)

1 sausage, cut into bite-sized pieces

3 tablespoons mixed vegetables

3 tablespoons chopped onions

1 tablespoon ketchup

1 egg

1 tablespoon milk

½ tablespoon butter

salt to taste

1 teaspoon pepper

Instructions: Makes 1 serving.

1. Make the ketchup rice. In a microwave-safe bowl, mix the rice, sausage, mixed vegetables, onions, and ketchup. Microwave for 1 minute.

2. Add the rice, ½ tablespoon of butter, and a little salt and pepper. Mix the ingredients together and microwave for another 2 minutes.

3. Place the ketchup rice on a plate and leave a 2¼- to 2½-inch opening in the middle.

4. Make the omelet. Whisk the egg in a bowl, mixing in the milk and a little salt.

5. Place plastic wrap in a round bowl or lightly oil the bowl and then add the egg mixture. Microwave for 30 seconds to 1 minute, until cooked through.

6. Add 1 teaspoon of butter on top of the egg and microwave for an additional 15 to 20 seconds.

7. Flip the omelet over in the middle of the ketchup rice. Shape it into a ball.

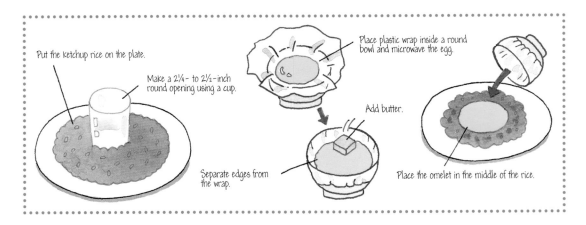

Put the ketchup rice on the plate.

Make a 2¼- to 2½-inch round opening using a cup.

Separate edges from the wrap.

Place plastic wrap inside a round bowl and microwave the egg.

Add butter.

Place the omelet in the middle of the rice.

Psyduck

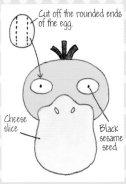

Cut off the rounded ends of the egg.
Cheese slice
Black sesame seed

Ingredients:

Cheese slice, quail egg (or hard-boiled egg), nori (dried seaweed), black sesame seed, tonkatsu sauce (a mix of Worcestershire sauce and ketchup may be substituted)

Instructions:

1. Cut the round ends off the egg and place them where the eyes will be. Put a black sesame seed in the middle of the egg for each eyeball.
2. Cut the cheese slice in the shape of the bill. Use a small spoon to make the nostrils. Brush the sauce on.
3. Cut the nori into small strips to make the hair.

Pikachu

Add sauce.
Cheese slice
Carrot
Raisins

Ingredients:

Cheese slice, raisins, thinly sliced carrots, tonkatsu sauce

Instructions:

1. Cut the cheese slice in the shape of its ears and place them on the rice. Use the sauce to color in the tips of the ears.
2. Add a little water to the thinly sliced carrots and microwave for 1 minute. Cut them into circles and place on the cheeks.
3. Make the eyes and mouth with raisins.

Sunflora

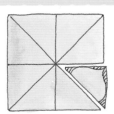

Cut the cheese slice as shown. You will make eight flower petals.

Ingredients:

Cheese slice, thinly sliced carrot, raisins, spinach, tonkatsu sauce

Instructions:

1. Make the flower petals out of the cheese slice.
2. Add a little water to the thinly sliced carrot and microwave for 1 minute. Cut the carrot into the shape of the mouth and place it on the omelet. Make the eyes out of raisins.
3. Cut the omelet to make the face lines, and put tonkatsu sauce in the lines.
4. Make the hands and body with the spinach leaves.

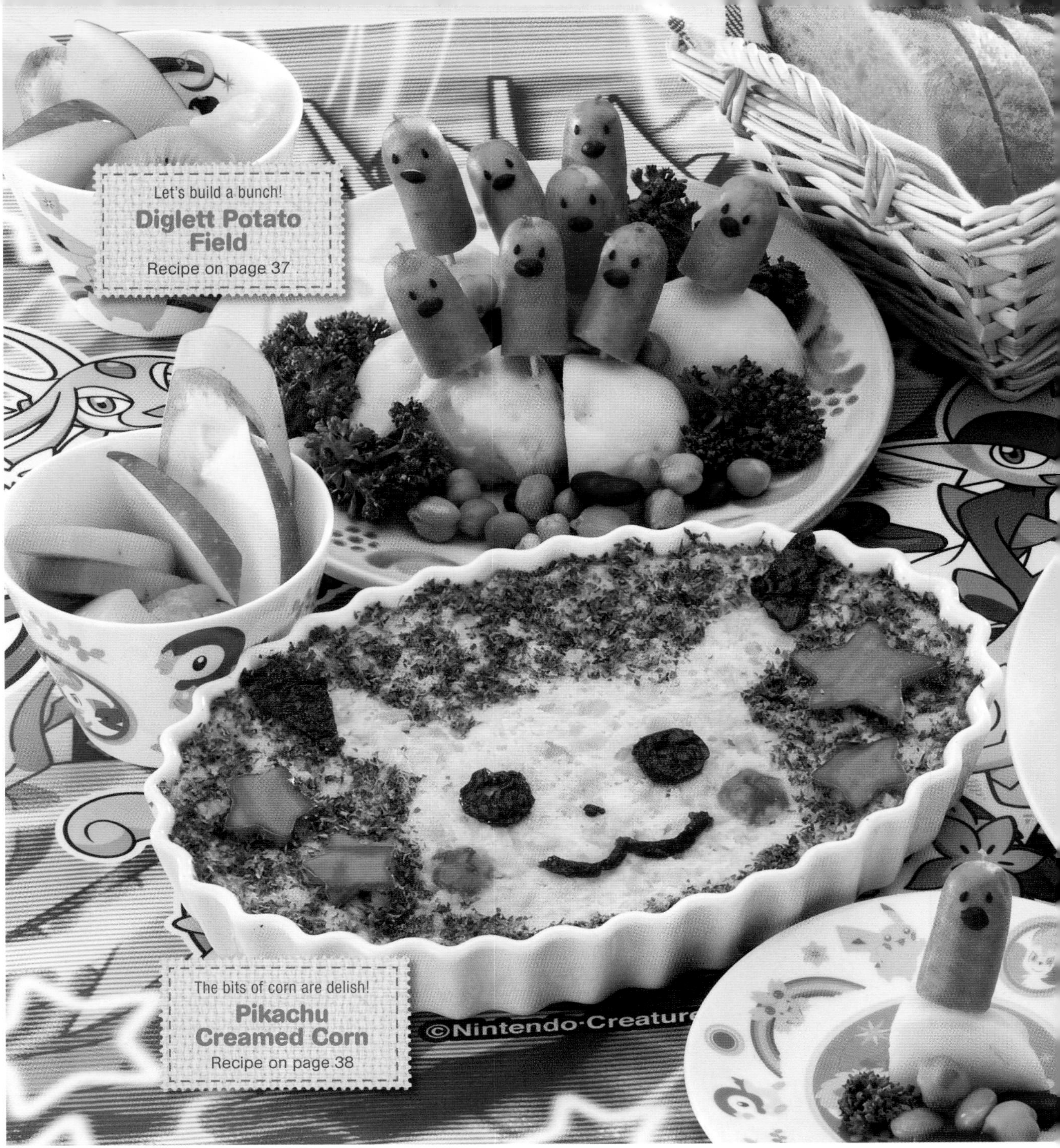
©Nintendo·Creature

Let's build a bunch!

Diglett Potato Field

Recipe on page 37

The bits of corn are delish!

Pikachu Creamed Corn

Recipe on page 38

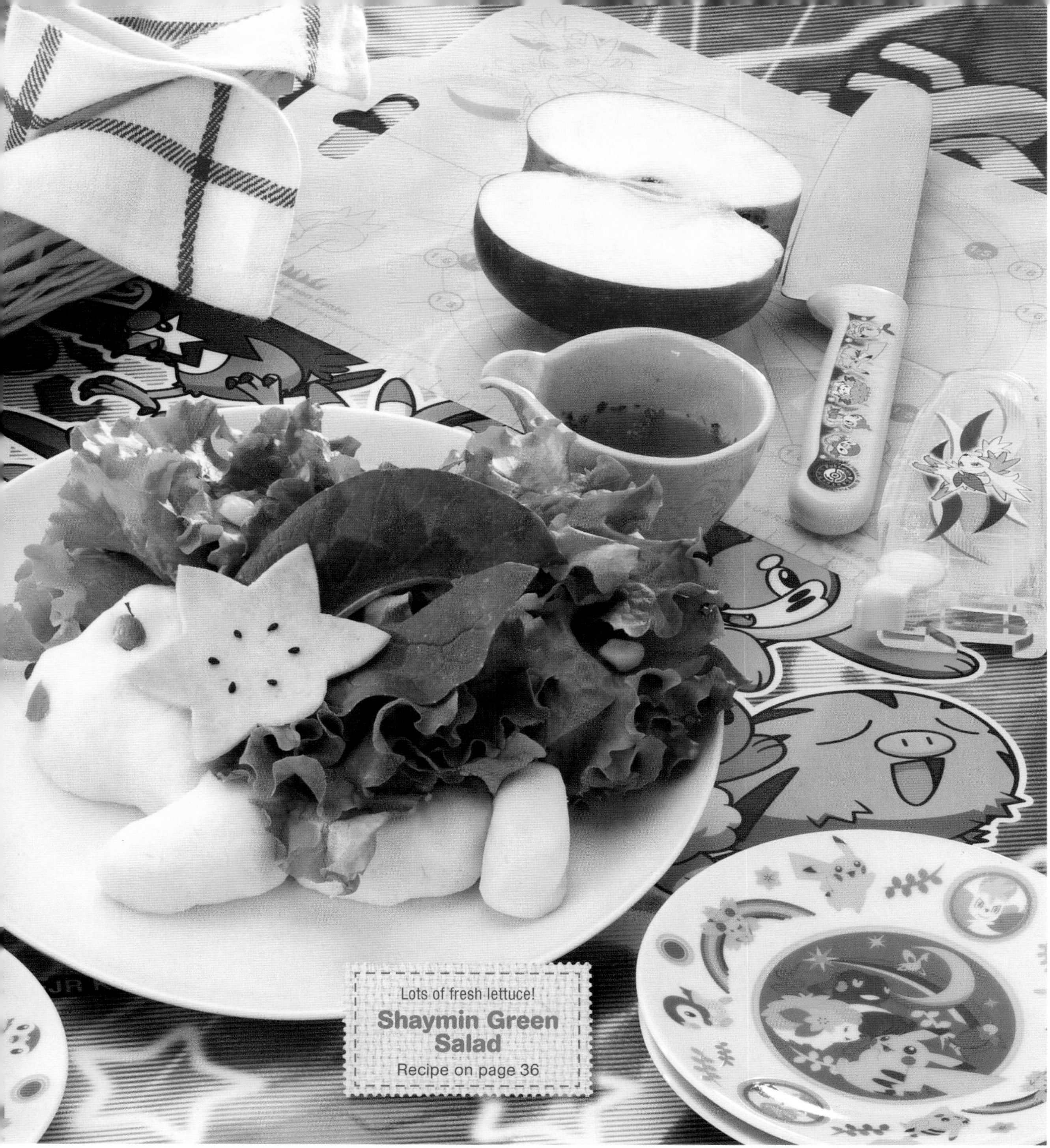

Lots of fresh lettuce!

Shaymin Green Salad

Recipe on page 36

Shaymin Green Salad Page 35

You can make Land Forme Shaymin with mashed potatoes and green-leaf lettuce. Add salad dressing or mayonnaise if you like.

★ ★

Ingredients:

½ head green-leaf lettuce

2 ounces mashed potato mix

4 tablespoons milk

10 tablespoons warm water

1 slice ham

1 spinach leaf

1 green pea

1 carrot

10–12 corn kernels, to taste

7 black sesame seeds

Instructions: Makes 1–2 servings.

1. Mix the mashed potato mix, warm water, and milk in a bowl to make the mashed potatoes. If consistency is too thick, add a little more water.

2. Shape the mashed potatoes into Shaymin's body and place on a plate.

3. Tear off the leaves of the green-leaf lettuce to make Shaymin's body.

4. Use the ham (cut in a flower shape), spinach, green pea, carrot, and sesame seeds to complete Shaymin's head as shown in the illustration. Add corn kernels to salad.

Helpful Hint

You can also microwave a potato and mash it to make the mashed potatoes. See the instructions on page 37 to make it this way.

Gratitude Pokémon
Shaymin

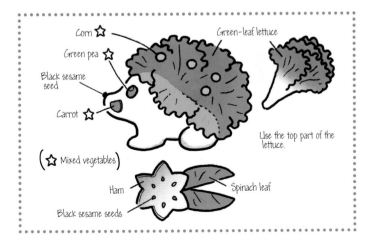

Corn ☆

Green pea ☆

Black sesame seed

Carrot ☆

Green-leaf lettuce

Use the top part of the lettuce.

(☆ Mixed vegetables)

Ham

Black sesame seeds

Spinach leaf

Diglett Potato Field

Page 34

Hot dogs and potatoes go great together! Use a mix of beans for added decoration.

Ingredients:

- 2 large potatoes
- 5–6 hot dogs
- mixed beans of your choice for decoration (red kidney beans, garbanzo beans, and peas recommended)
- 4 red kidney beans
- 12–16 black sesame seeds
- ⅙ teaspoon ketchup

Helpful Hint

There are many different types of potatoes—Russet, Yukon Gold, Irish Cobbler—that make fluffy potatoes.

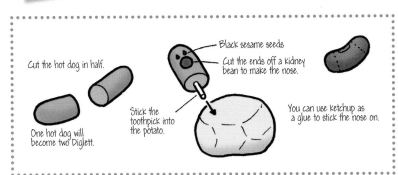

Instructions: Makes 3–4 servings.

1. Wash the potatoes thoroughly and wrap them in a paper towel. Microwave for 5 minutes until soft. Stick a toothpick in the potatoes to see whether the insides are soft.
2. Once the potatoes are cool to the touch, peel the skin off and cut into wedges. Place the potatoes on a plate.
3. Boil some water in a pan and cook the hot dogs. Remove them from the water and cut each one in half.
4. Stick one end of a toothpick into the hot dog and the other end into the potato.
5. Use the red kidney beans and black sesame seeds to create Diglett's face. Add mixed beans to the plate for decoration.

Cut the hot dog in half.
One hot dog will become two Diglett.
Stick the toothpick into the potato.
Black sesame seeds
Cut the ends off a kidney bean to make the nose.
You can use ketchup as a glue to stick the nose on.

Mole Pokémon
Diglett

Pikachu Creamed Corn

Page 34

A baked dish that smells like butter and has sweet bits of corn. You can make it without using a knife.

★ ★

Ingredients:

7 ounces canned whole-kernel corn

3 tablespoons wheat flour

1½ tablespoons butter

1 egg

6¾ ounces milk

3⅓ tablespoons sugar

pinch of salt

¼ cup dried, chopped parsley

2 prunes

1 teaspoon ketchup

Instructions: Makes 2–3 servings.

1. Preheat oven to 350°F.

2. Drain the water from the canned corn and place the corn in a bowl with the flour.

3. Melt the butter in the microwave and then mix it with the corn.

4. In a separate bowl, mix the egg, milk, sugar, and salt.

5. In a baking dish, spread out the corn so that it is flat. Pour the egg and milk mixture over the corn. Bake in the oven for 10 minutes.

6. When the ingredients start to rise, cover the dish with aluminum foil and bake for another 15 to 20 minutes. If nothing sticks to the toothpick when you pull it out, it's done.

7. Place a piece of paper that has been cut in the shape of Pikachu's head on top of the creamed corn. Sprinkle parsley around the paper.

8. Remove the paper and create Pikachu's face with prunes and ketchup.

Use a colander to drain the water.

Wheat flour

Sugar

Egg

Milk

Melted butter

Salt

Mix thoroughly before pouring over corn.

Final Touch

Parsley

Shake the parsley over the paper cutout.

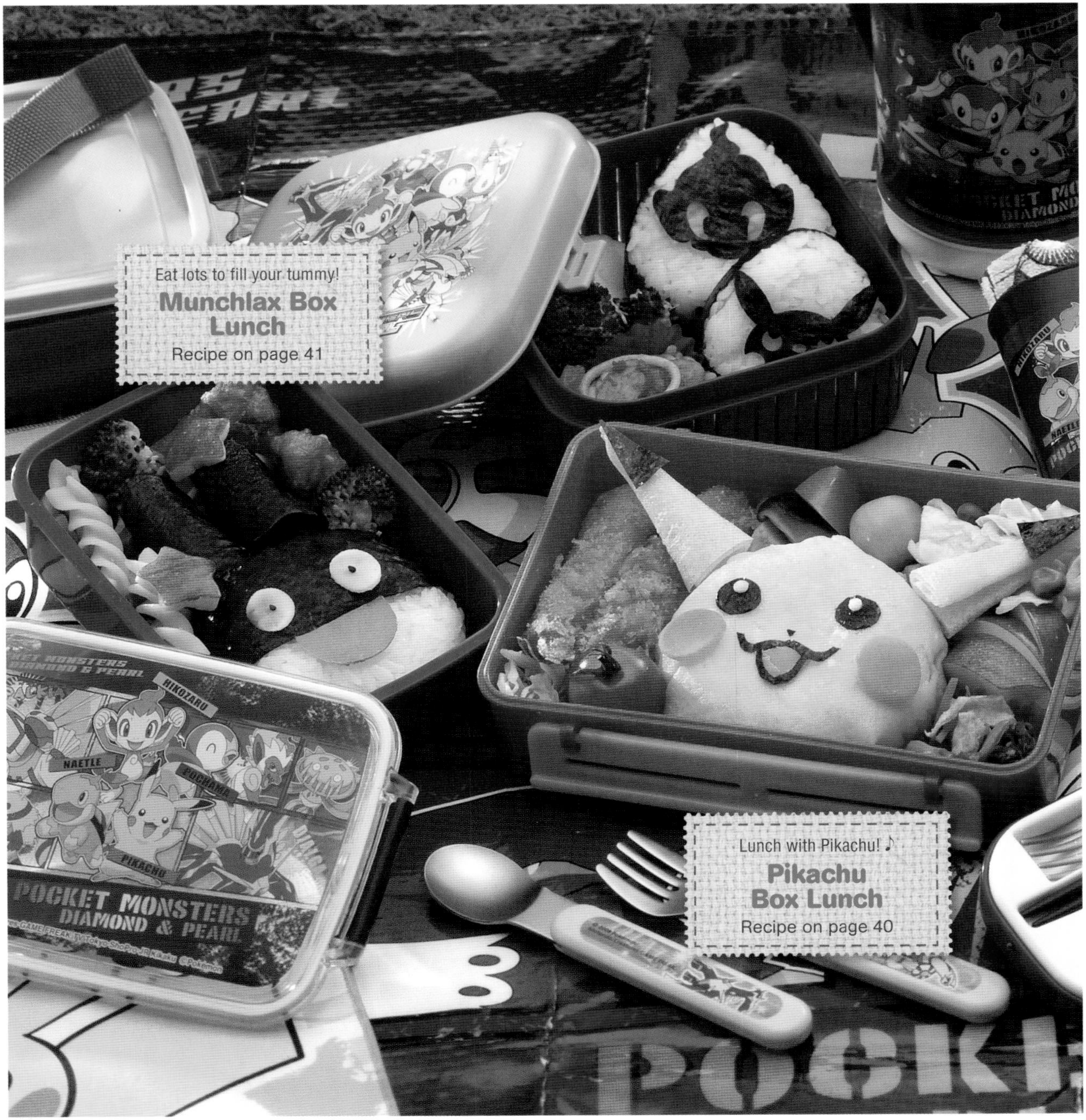
POCKET MONSTERS
DIAMOND & PEARL
HIKOZARU
NAETLE
PUCHAMA
PIKACHU
POCKET MONSTERS
DIAMOND & PEARL

Eat lots to fill your tummy!

Munchlax Box Lunch

Recipe on page 41

Lunch with Pikachu! ♪

Pikachu Box Lunch

Recipe on page 40

Page 39

Pikachu Box Lunch

Wrap an egg crepe around some rice to make Pikachu. Be sure to eat all your veggies!

★ ★

Ingredients:

1 cup cooked rice (short-grain Japanese sticky rice recommended)

1 egg

1 teaspoon sugar

1 teaspoon vegetable oil

1 teaspoon cornstarch, mixed with 1 teaspoon water

2 slices carrot, about 1 inch in diameter

1 slice kamaboko (fish cake), or substitute daikon radish or water chestnuts

1 sheet nori (dried seaweed)

Instructions: Makes 1 serving.

1. Whisk the egg in a bowl and strain it with a metal sieve. Mix in 1 teaspoon of sugar, 1 teaspoon of vegetable oil, and 1 teaspoon of cornstarch (that has been mixed with 1 teaspoon of water).

2. Wrap a large plate with plastic wrap and spread out the egg mixture in a 6-inch circle. Microwave for 30 seconds to 1 minute. When all of the egg has hardened, remove it from the microwave and peel it off the plastic wrap. Repeat.

3. Place the egg crepe on top of a sheet of plastic wrap. Form a ball with the rice and wrap the egg and plastic wrap around it. Set aside.

4. Cut the other egg crepe in half. Fold it as shown in the illustration to make two ears.

5. Remove the plastic wrap from the egg-covered rice and place it inside a lunch box. Fill the box with other food before adding the ears.

6. Add a little water to the carrot slices and microwave for 1 minute. Create Pikachu's face with the carrots, kamaboko, and nori.

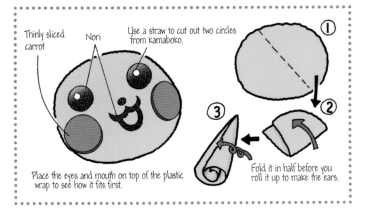

Thinly sliced carrot

Nori

Use a straw to cut out two circles from kamaboko.

Place the eyes and mouth on top of the plastic wrap to see how it fits first.

① ② ③

Fold it in half before you roll it up to make the ears.

Munchlax Box Lunch

Page 39

Just wrap some nori around a rice ball to make the always-hungry Munchlax. Fill the rest of the box with some tasty food!

Ingredients:

- 1 cup cooked rice (short-grain Japanese sticky rice recommended)
- ½ fish sausage, or substitute other sausage or hot dog
- ½ sheet nori (dried seaweed)
- 1 piece thinly sliced carrot
- 2 thin slices kamaboko (fish cake), or substitute daikon radish or water chestnuts
- black sesame seeds

Helpful Hint

If you're using hot rice, first place it in a bowl and lightly roll it around until it cools a bit. Then you can roll it in your hands.

Instructions: Makes 1 serving.

1. Make a big rice ball.
2. Wrap nori around the top half of the rice ball.
3. Cut the fish sausage in half diagonally. Wrap nori around each piece.
4. Place the rice ball inside a lunch box. Fill the box with other food before adding the fish sausage.
5. Add a little water to the thinly sliced carrot and microwave for 1 minute. Create Munchlax's face with the carrot, fish cake, and sesame seeds.

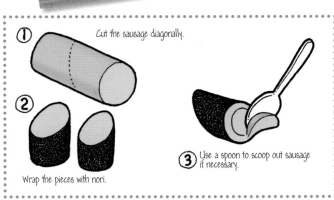

①
Cut the sausage diagonally.
②
Wrap the pieces with nori.
③
Use a spoon to scoop out sausage if necessary.

Big Eater Pokémon
Munchlax

A lovely teatime treat!

Burmy Three-Colored Mochi

Recipe on page 46

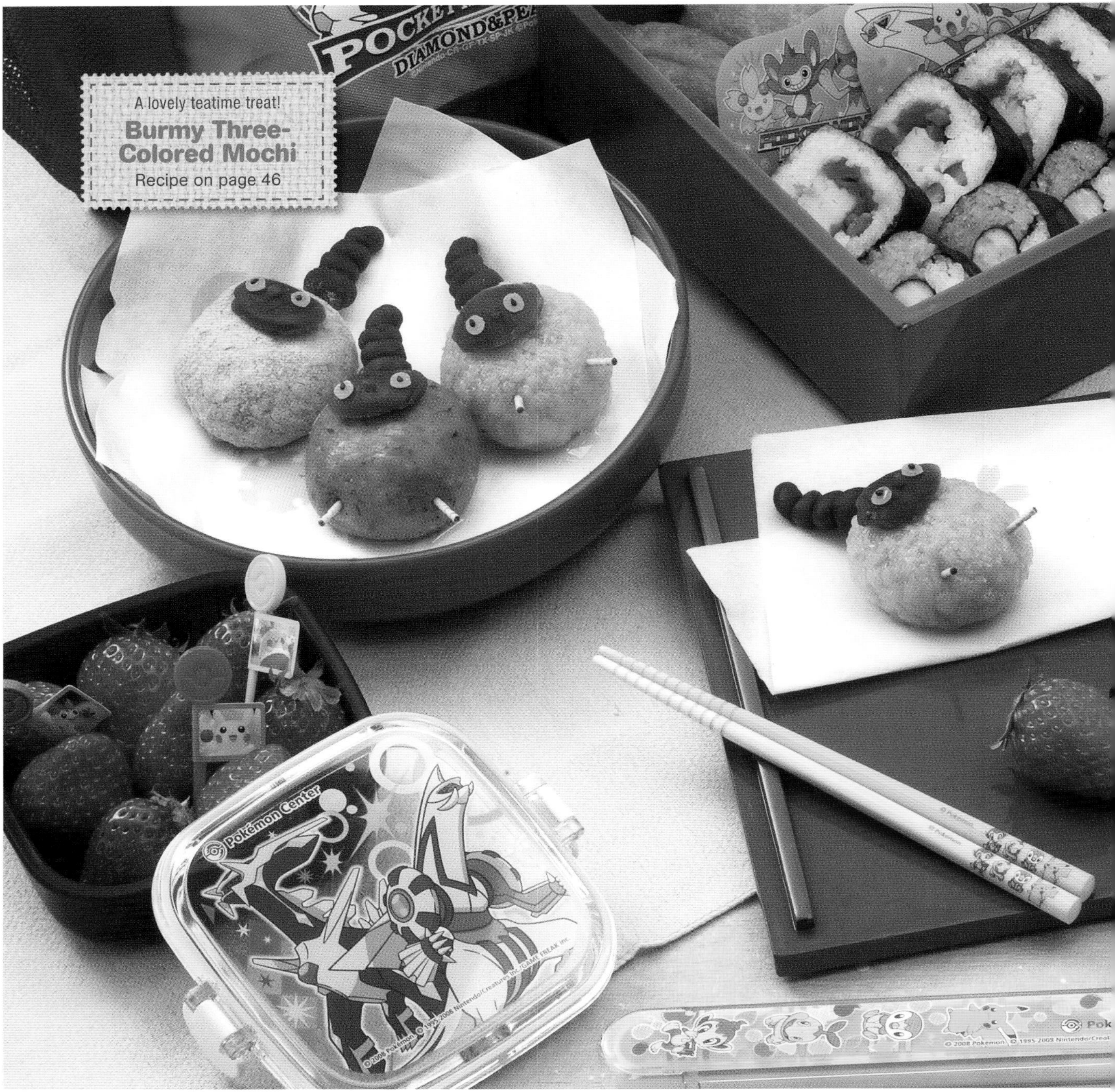
Pokémon Center

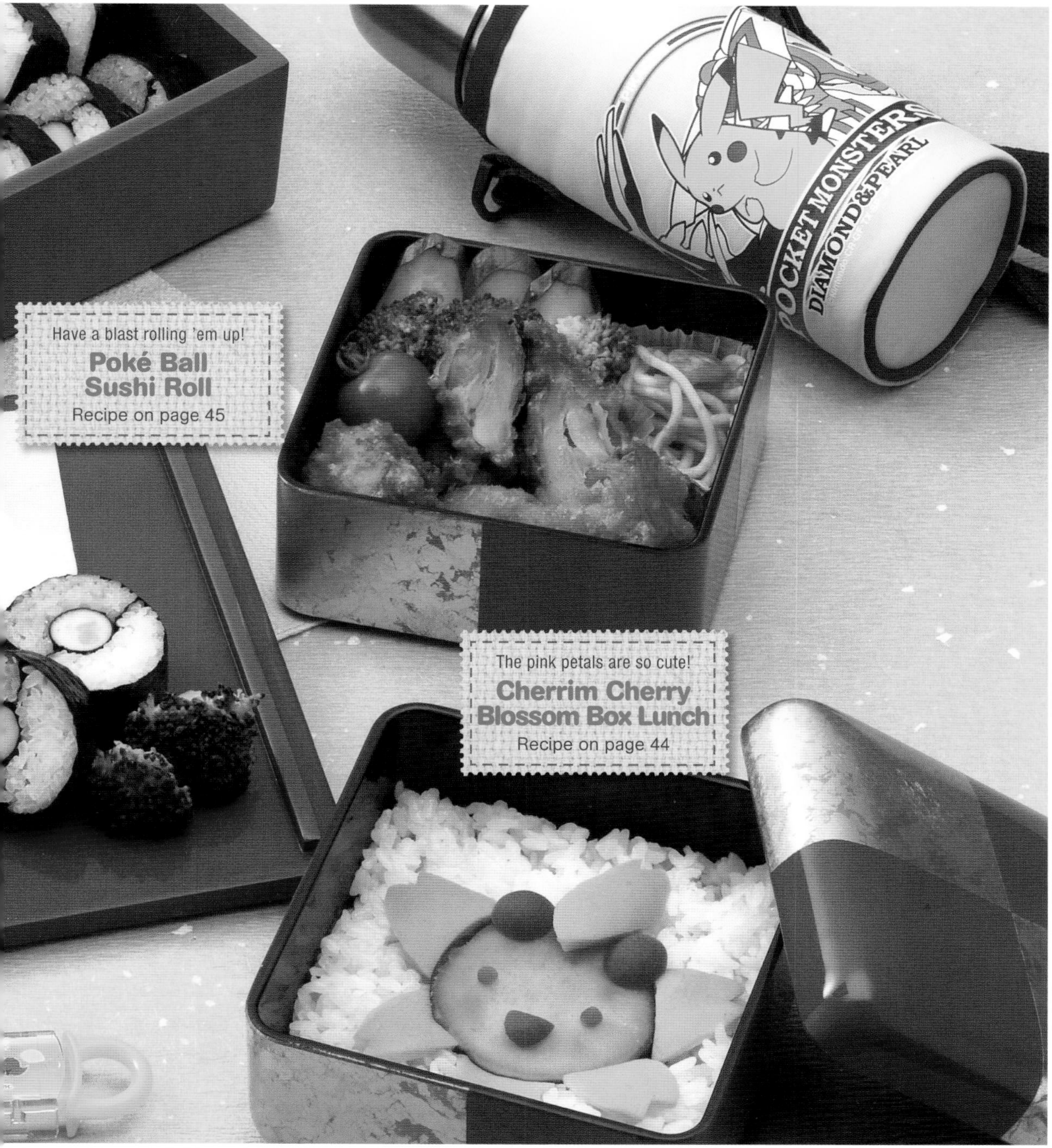
POCKET MONSTERS
DIAMOND&PEARL

Have a blast rolling 'em up!

Poké Ball Sushi Roll

Recipe on page 45

The pink petals are so cute!

Cherrim Cherry Blossom Box Lunch

Recipe on page 44

Cherrim Cherry Blossom Box Lunch

Page 43

Open the box to see Cherrim smiling back at you! You'll always be in a flower-viewing mood with this box lunch. There's also sweet potato inside.

★ ★

Ingredients:

1 bowl cooked rice (short-grain Japanese sticky rice recommended)

1 slice sweet potato, ½ inch wide

2 tablespoons sugar

pinch of salt

½ pink kamaboko (fish cake), or substitute daikon radish or water chestnuts

1 salted plum

Instructions: Makes 1 serving.

1. Cut a ½-inch-wide slice of sweet potato and let it sit in water for 10 minutes.

2. Put the sweet potato in a pot with enough water to cover it, and heat.

3. After 3 minutes, add 2 tablespoons of sugar and a pinch of salt. On low heat, simmer until the sweet potato is soft.

4. Place the sweet potato in a lunch box and fill the remaining space with rice.

5. Create Cherrim's face with the pink part of the fish cake and the salted plums.

Helpful Hint

Add 1 tablespoon of soy sauce to the leftover sweet potato and stew it for 2 to 3 minutes to create a dish that goes well with rice.

Blossom Pokémon
Cherrim

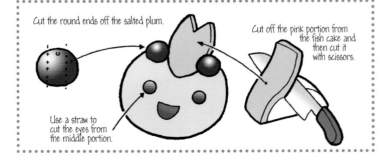

Cut the round ends off the salted plum.

Cut off the pink portion from the fish cake and then cut it with scissors.

Use a straw to cut the eyes from the middle portion.

Poké Ball Sushi Roll

Page 43

This sushi roll looks like a Poké Ball when cut. The more times you make it, the better you'll get!

★ ★

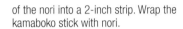

Ingredients:

1 cup cooked sushi rice

sushi rice seasoning (see Helpful Hint on page 48)

tarako (salted cod roe) furikake seasoning*

2 stick-type kamaboko (fish cake)

1 sheet + 2 inches nori (dried seaweed)

Furikake are dry seasoning flakes that you put on top of rice.

Instructions: Makes 1 sushi roll.

1. Split the rice into two portions. Mix one portion with the sushi rice seasoning and the other with the tarako furikake seasoning.

2. Cut the kamaboko stick to match the length of the nori sheet. Cut the width of the nori into a 2-inch strip. Wrap the kamaboko stick with nori.

3. Cut the 2-inch nori strip in half as shown in the illustration and fold in two.

4. Place a sheet of nori on a bamboo sushi rolling mat, and spread the two types of rice as shown in the illustration. Place the kamaboko stick in the middle.

5. Start rolling from the side closest to you. Once rolled, set aside for a while with the flap at the bottom.

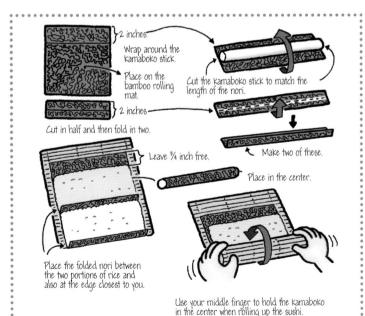

2 inches

Wrap around the kamaboko stick.

Place on the bamboo rolling mat.

Cut the kamaboko stick to match the length of the nori.

2 inches

Cut in half and then fold in two.

Make two of these.

Leave ¾ inch free.

Place in the center.

Place the folded nori between the two portions of rice and also at the edge closest to you.

Use your middle finger to hold the kamaboko in the center when rolling up the sushi.

Burmy Three-Colored Mochi

Page 42

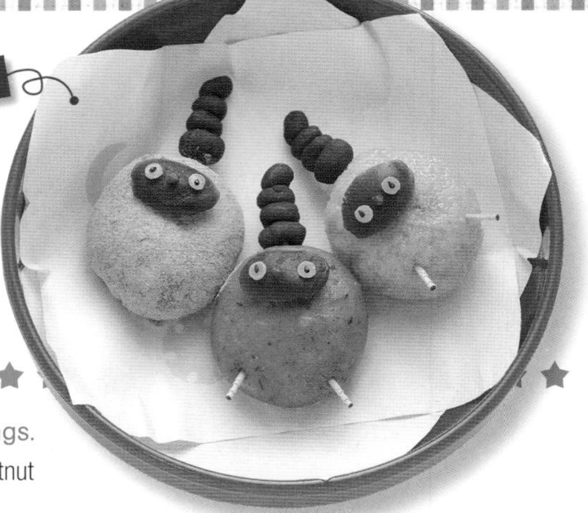

You can make three different Burmy from store-bought traditional Japanese sweets. Pour yourself a cup of tea and enjoy the flavors.

Ingredients:

1 sakura mochi*

2 kusa mochi**

1 slice chestnut yokan***

sprinkle of kinako (soybean) powder

6 black sesame seeds

Instructions: Makes 3 servings.

1. Use a spoon to scoop out the chestnut yokan to make three faces.
2. Add a little water to 1 tablespoon of chestnut yokan and microwave for 10 seconds.
3. Mash the microwaved chestnut yokan with a fork and make them into balls (small, medium, large). Make three sets.
4. Sprinkle kinako powder on one of the kusa mochi.
5. Make the face with a thinly sliced chestnut and black sesame seeds. Insert the rolled balls on top of each mochi to make the head.

**Sakura (cherry blossom) mochi is filled with red beans.*
***Kusa (grass) mochi is mixed with fibers from the yomogi (mugwort) plant.*
****Yokan is a hardened azuki (red bean) jelly brick.*

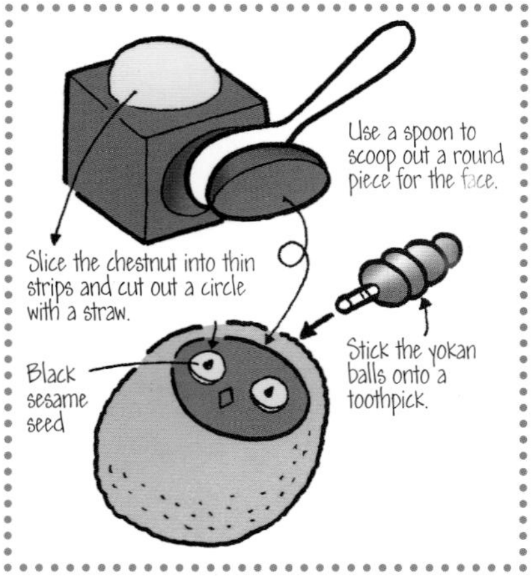
Use a spoon to scoop out a round piece for the face.
Slice the chestnut into thin strips and cut out a circle with a straw.
Black sesame seed
Stick the yokan balls onto a toothpick.

If you can't find these ingredients at an Asian grocery store, you can get creative and substitute doughnut holes for the mochi and chocolate for the yokan. Brush food coloring on the doughnuts to achieve desired colors.

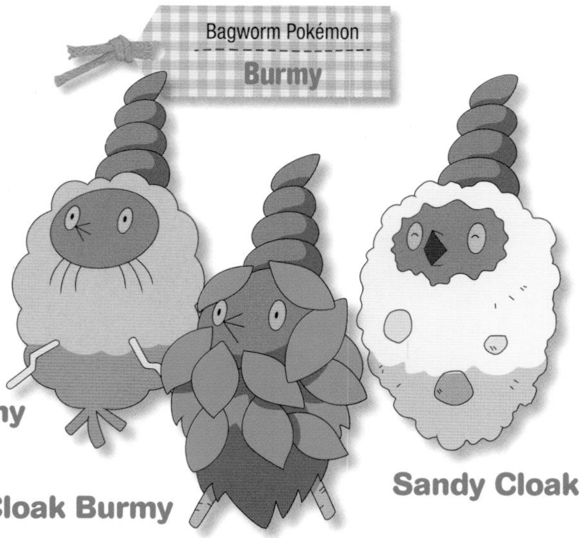
Bagworm Pokémon
Burmy

Trash Cloak Burmy

Plant Cloak Burmy

Sandy Cloak Burmy

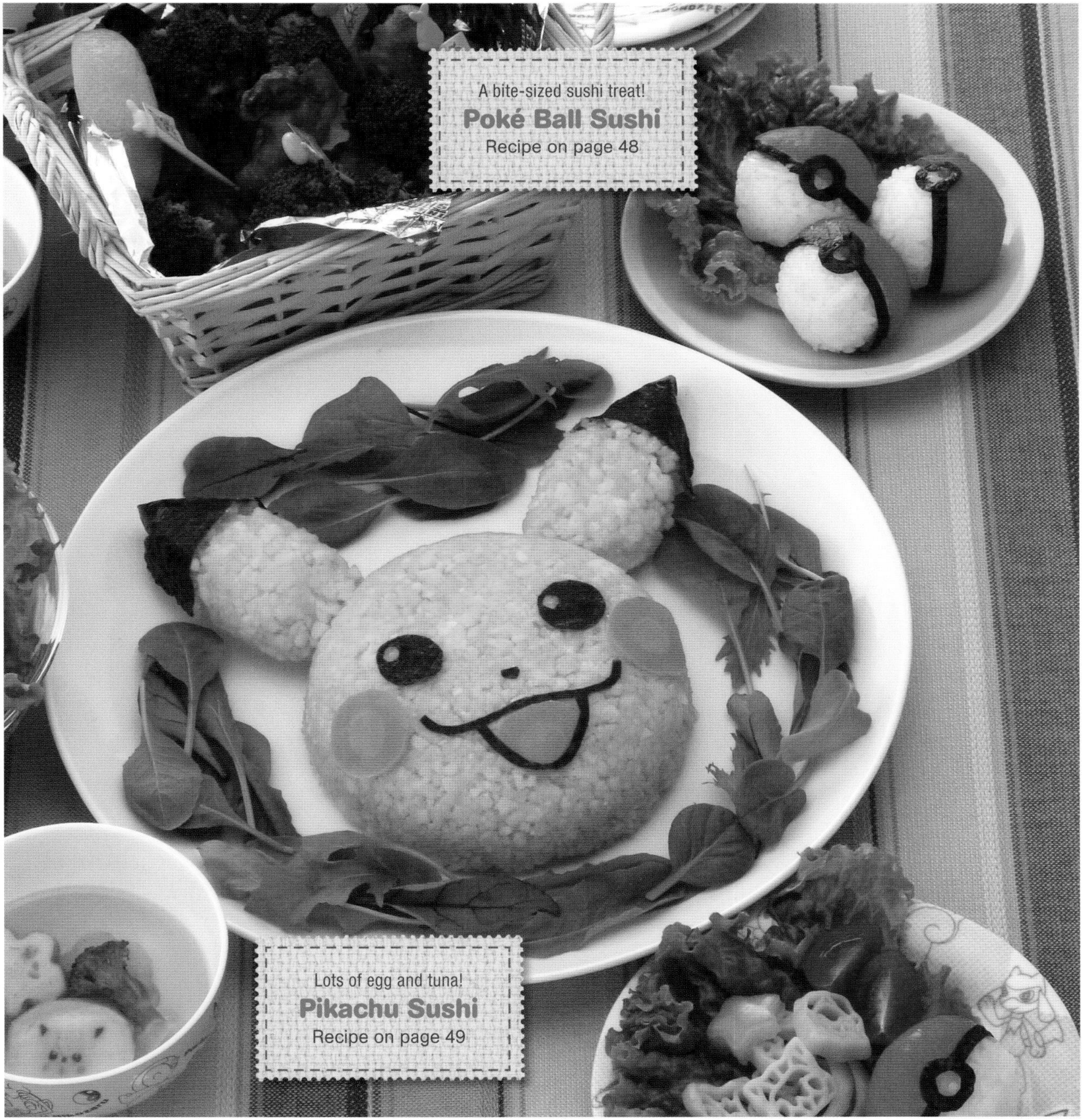

A bite-sized sushi treat!

Poké Ball Sushi

Recipe on page 48

Lots of egg and tuna!

Pikachu Sushi

Recipe on page 49

Poké Ball Sushi

Place red smoked salmon over white rice and round it into a ball. The nori decoration is the key!

Page 47

★ ★

Ingredients:

1 cup cooked rice (short-grain Japanese sticky rice recommended)

sushi rice seasoning (see Helpful Hint)

½ pack smoked salmon

1–2 sheets nori (dried seaweed)

Instructions: Makes 4 servings.

1. Add the sushi rice seasoning to the cooked rice to make sushi rice.

2. Make 4 round rice balls.

3. Put plastic wrap on a plate and place the smoked salmon on it. Put the rice ball on top and wrap the salmon around the ball. Place it so that the salmon covers only half of the ball. If the salmon is covering too much, trim it with some scissors.

4. Remove the plastic wrap from the rice ball. Cut the nori and place it on the rice ball to form the center decoration.

Helpful Hint

If you don't have sushi rice seasoning, create your own! Mix 1 tablespoon of vinegar, 2 teaspoons of sugar, and ⅓ teaspoon of salt together. Then mix it into hot sushi rice.

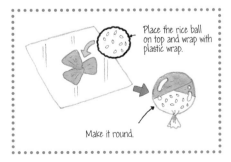

Place the rice ball on top and wrap with plastic wrap.

Make it round.

Pikachu Sushi

Page 47

Make Pikachu sushi by using a round container to shape its face. You can make the egg easily in the microwave.

★ ★ ★ ★ ★ ★ ★ ★ ★ ★ ★ ★ ★ ★ ★ ★ ★ ★ ★ ★

Ingredients:

3 cups cooked rice (short-grain Japanese sticky rice recommended)

sushi rice seasoning (see Helpful Hint on page 48)

3 eggs

1 6-ounce can tuna

3 pieces thinly sliced carrot

½ sheet nori (dried seaweed)

1 tablespoon soy sauce

1 tablespoon sugar

pinch of salt

Instructions: Makes 3–4 servings.

1. Add the sushi rice seasoning to the cooked rice to make sushi rice.

2. In a microwave-safe bowl, mix the eggs and a pinch of salt.

3. Scramble the eggs in a frying pan on a stove top. Or microwave the eggs for 30 seconds to 1 minute, use a whisk to mix, and repeat a few times until you have scrambled eggs.

4. Drain the liquid from the tuna can. Mix the tuna with 1 tablespoon of soy sauce and 1 tablespoon of sugar.

5. Microwave the tuna for 2 minutes. Stir the tuna so the flakes are separated.

6. Make the ears: Take 1 tablespoon of the scrambled eggs and spread it on some plastic wrap. Make a long, skinny shape out of the sushi rice and place it on top of the egg. Wrap the entire rice portion and make it into an ear shape. Repeat to make the second ear.

7. Place plastic wrap inside a round bowl. Press down the remaining egg into the bowl. Then add a layer of sushi rice.

8. Squeeze out any excess liquid from the tuna and place it over the rice. Add the remaining sushi rice on top. Place something heavy on top so that the rice, tuna, and egg are pressed together.

9. Flip the bowl over and place the contents on a plate. Add the ears.

10 Add a little water to the thinly sliced carrots and microwave for 1 minute. Create Pikachu's face with the carrots and nori.

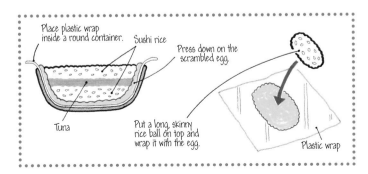

Place plastic wrap inside a round container.

Sushi rice

Press down on the scrambled egg.

Tuna

Put a long, skinny rice ball on top and wrap it with the egg.

Plastic wrap

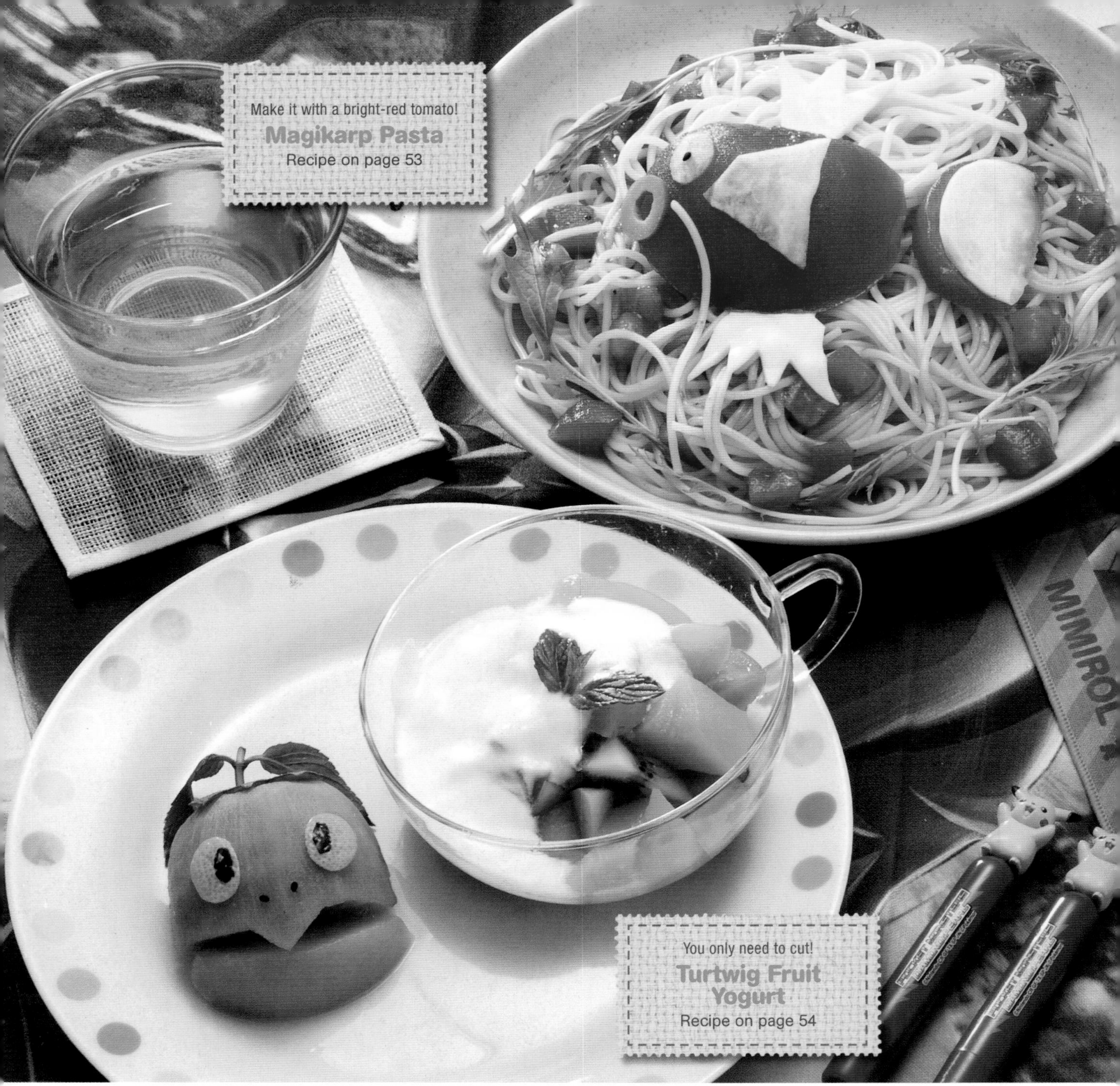
Make it with a bright-red tomato!
Magikarp Pasta
Recipe on page 53
MIMIROL
You only need to cut!
Turtwig Fruit Yogurt
Recipe on page 54

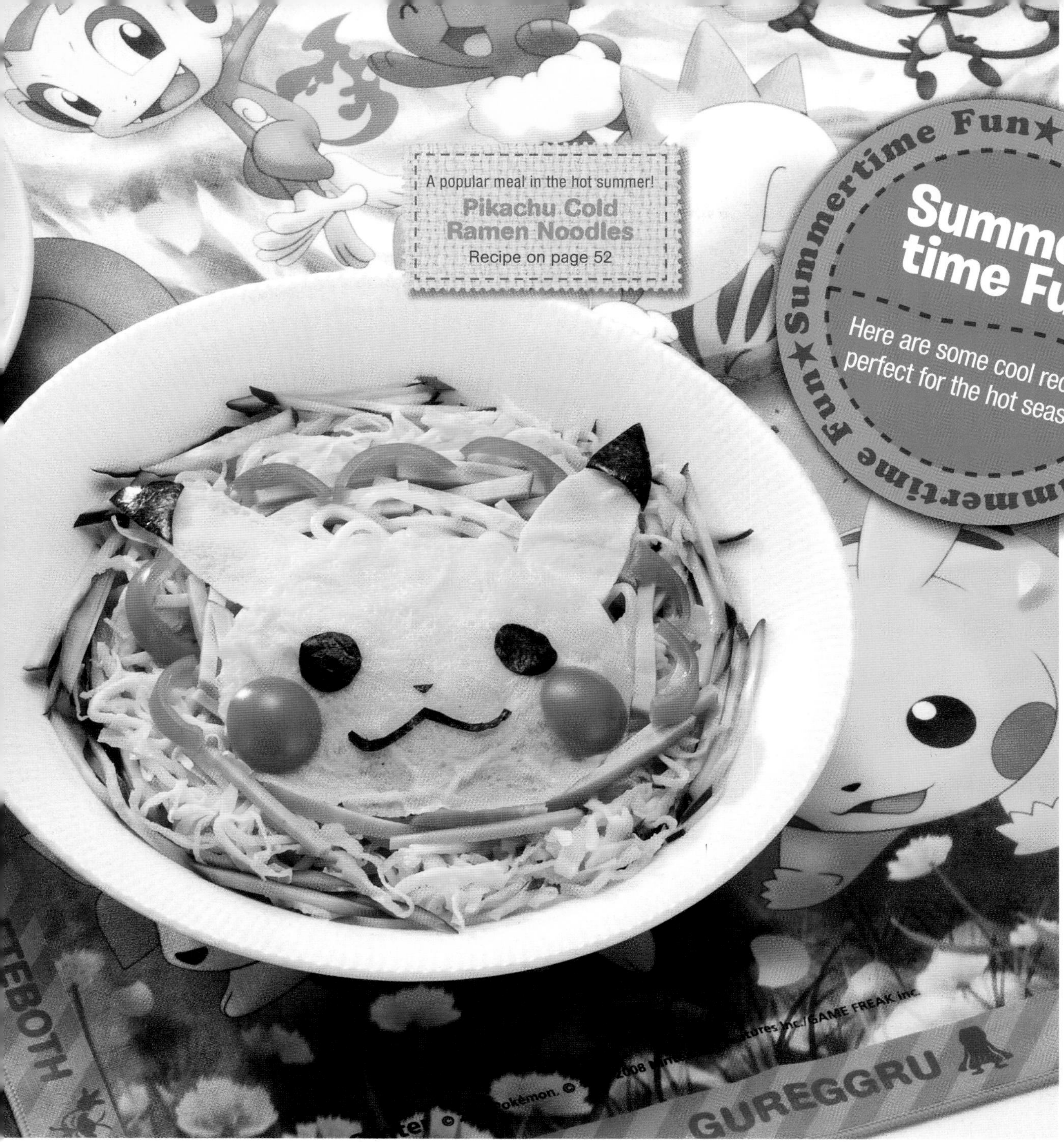
GUREGGRU

Summertime Fun

Here are some cool recipes perfect for the hot season!

A popular meal in the hot summer!

Pikachu Cold Ramen Noodles

Recipe on page 52

Pikachu Cold Ramen Noodles

Page 51

Top cold ramen noodles with an egg crepe of Pikachu's face. Not only is it fun to look at, it's good for you too!

★ ★

Ingredients:

2 packages store-bought ramen noodles

1 egg

1 cucumber

1 slice ham

2 cherry tomatoes

1 sheet nori (dried seaweed)

1 teaspoon sugar

1 teaspoon cornstarch, mixed with 1 teaspoon water

1 teaspoon vegetable oil

Instructions: Makes 2 servings.

1. Whisk the egg in a bowl and strain it with a metal sieve. Mix in 1 teaspoon of sugar, 1 teaspoon of vegetable oil, and the cornstarch and water mixture.

2. Wrap a large plate with plastic wrap and spread out the egg mixture in a 6-inch circle. Microwave for 30 seconds to 1 minute. When all of the egg has hardened, remove it from the microwave and peel it off the plastic wrap.

3. Cut out Pikachu's face and ears from one of the egg crepes. Slice the leftover egg crepe into thin strips. Repeat with the other egg crepe.

4. Julienne the cucumber and ham. Cut the cherry tomatoes vertically.

5. Boil the ramen noodles according to the instructions on the package. Chill with cold water and drain in a colander.

6. Put the ramen sauce (that's included with the noodles) onto a plate and place the noodles on top. Place the egg strips, cucumber, ham, sliced cherry tomatoes, and Pikachu's egg face on top of the noodles.

7. Make Pikachu's face with nori and cherry tomatoes.

Helpful Hint

Noodles will get stretched out if left too long after boiling. Get the toppings and sauce ready before boiling the noodles!

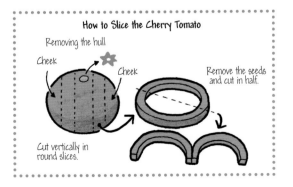

How to Slice the Cherry Tomato

Removing the hull

Cheek

Cheek

Remove the seeds and cut in half.

Cut vertically in round slices.

Magikarp Pasta

A cold pasta dish with tomatoes and fresh lemon sauce that's perfect for summer!

Page 50

★ ★

Ingredients:

4 ounces spaghetti (angel hair pasta recommended)

1 medium-sized tomato

1 tablespoon ketchup

1 tablespoon olive oil

1 teaspoon Worcestershire sauce

1 teaspoon lemon juice

½ teaspoon salt

pepper to taste

1 cheese slice

2 green olives

1 turnip

mustard greens for garnish

1 black sesame seed

Instructions: Makes 2 servings.

1. Remove the tomato hull and place the tomato in a ladle. Dunk in a pot of boiling water for 10 seconds. Remove and place in cold water. Peel off the skin.

2. Cut the tomato to create Magikarp's body and tail. Cut the remaining tomato into ⅓-inch cubes.

3. Mix the cubed tomatoes and the ketchup, olive oil, Worcestershire sauce, lemon juice, salt, and pepper in a bowl for the sauce.

4. Cut the olives in round slices. Set aside two slices for Magikarp's mouth and add the remainder to the sauce.

5. Boil the spaghetti and then cool it with water and drain.

6. Put the spaghetti on a plate, pour the sauce over it, and decorate with mustard greens. Place the tomato body and tail on top of the noodles. Finish Magikarp by making its fins and eyes out of the cheese slice, turnip, and black seasame seed.

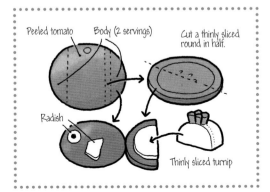

Peeled tomato   Body (2 servings)   Cut a thinly sliced round in half.

Radish

Thinly sliced turnip

Fish Pokémon
Magikarp

Turtwig Fruit Yogurt

Page 50

A Turtwig made from a green kiwi and a yellow peach.
A healthy dessert that's perfect after a meal.

Ingredients:

1 kiwi

2 slices canned peaches

½ cup plain yogurt

1 lemon peel

3–4 mint leaves

Instructions: Makes 2 servings.

1. Peel the skin off the kiwi. Cut it in half vertically and then cut it to form Turtwig's face.

2. Use one peach slice to make Turtwig's jaw.

3. Cut the lemon peel and the kiwi skin with scissors to make the eyes and head. Place the mint on top.

4. Cut the remaining kiwi and peaches into bite-sized pieces and place in a bowl. Add plain yogurt and the syrup from the canned peaches if you like.

5. Place mint leaves on Turtwig's head and add as garnish to fruit yogurt if desired.

Helpful Hint

Here's a tip for making cold dishes—put your plates and bowls in the refrigerator to chill. The cool taste will last longer!

Tiny Leaf Pokémon

Turtwig

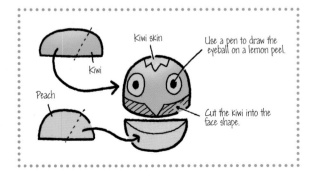

Kiwi skin

Kiwi

Peach

Use a pen to draw the eyeball on a lemon peel.

Cut the kiwi into the face shape.

Cooking Technique Lesson 2

How to Use Tools Wisely

The recipes in this book use a lot of different tools such as knives and kitchen scissors. Here are some other useful tools.

Spoons

When making Pokémon parts from cheese slices or thinly sliced vegetables that need to be curved, a spoon works better than a knife. Use a rounded spoon to press down little by little to cut. It's best to have a variety of spoon sizes ready.

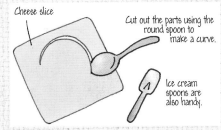

Cheese slice
Cut out the parts using the round spoon to make a curve.
Ice cream spoons are also handy.

Straws & Caps

Use these when making round eyes or even the white highlights in the eyes by punching out a hole. Cut the straw so it's about 1 inch long and push it down on the ingredient to make a hole. If you have one narrow straw and one wide straw, they'll come in handy.

You can even use a plastic bottle cap or small cup to punch out holes.
Push the straw down to make a hole.

Cookie Cutter

A cookie cutter is a metal cutter that can be used to make flowers or star shapes from vegetables or fruits. You can even use just part of the cutout to make a Pokémon part.

Flower cookie cutter
If you use just this portion, it becomes a heart!

Plastic Wrap

You'll use this when you need to make rice into a ball or to shape something into a Pokémon. When you wrap rice, press firmly to make the shapes.

Shape with your hands over the plastic wrap.

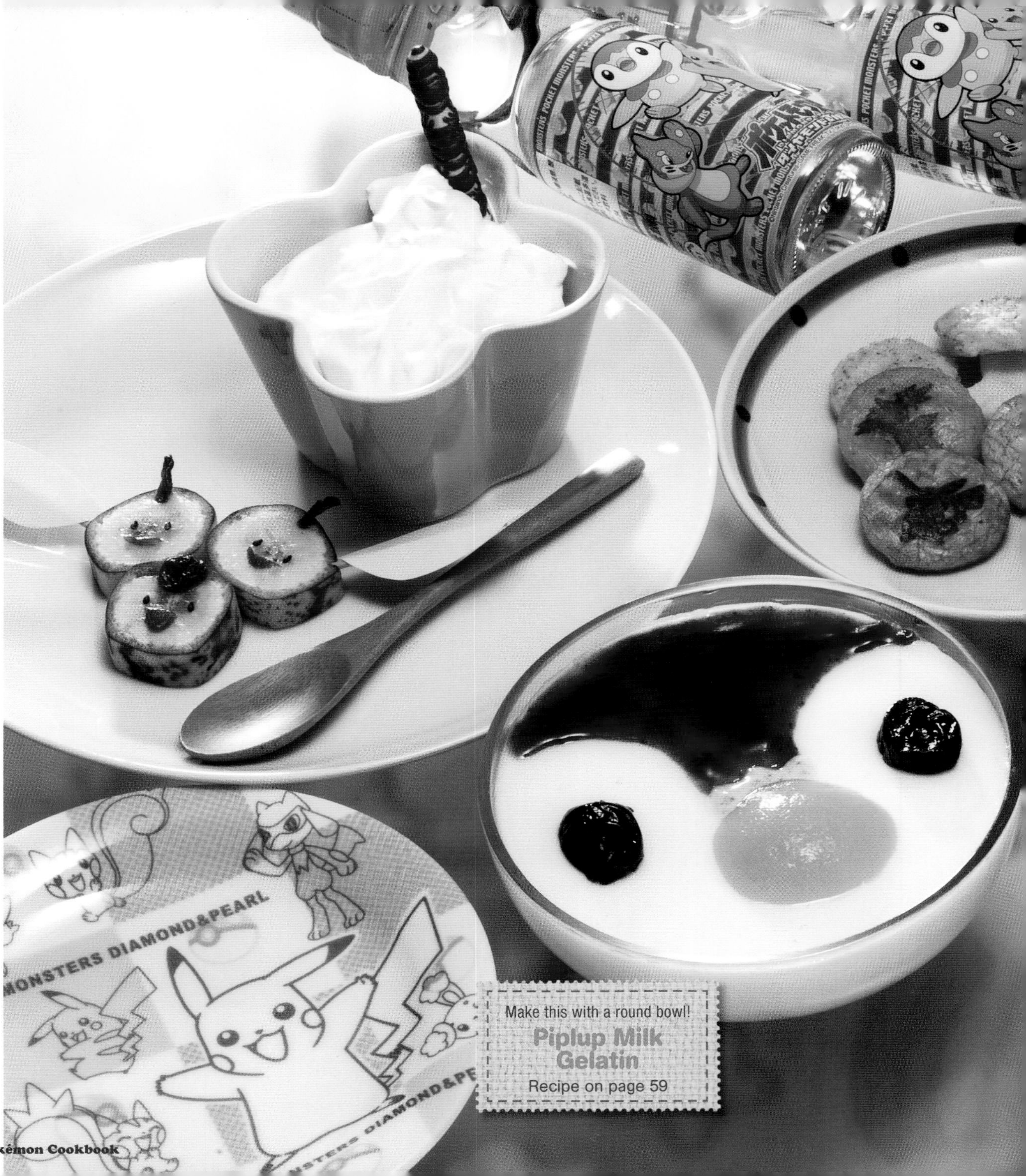
MONSTERS DIAMOND&PEARL

Make this with a round bowl!

Piplup Milk Gelatin

Recipe on page 59

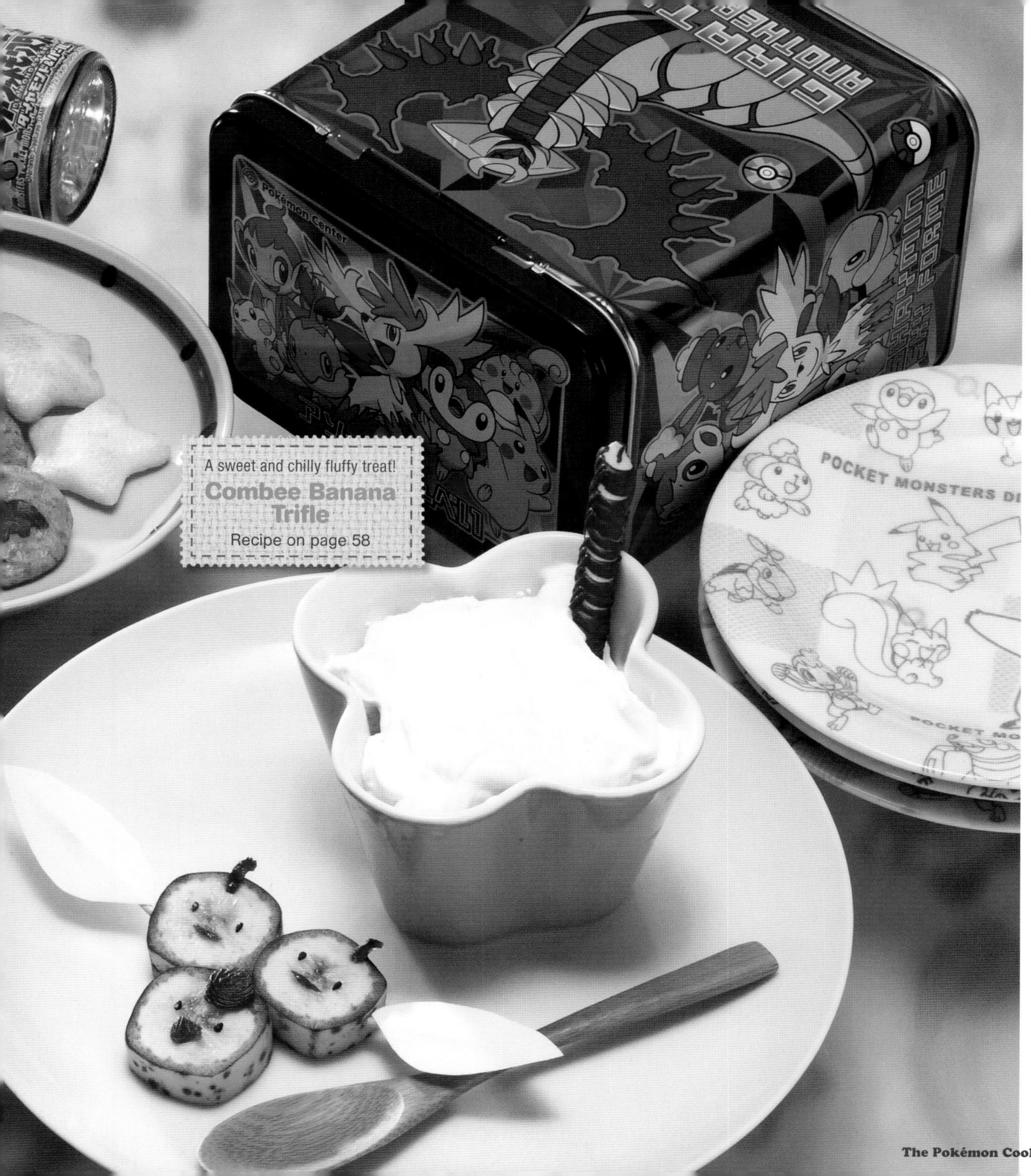
Pokémon Center

A sweet and chilly fluffy treat!

Combee Banana Trifle

Recipe on page 58

Combee Banana Trifle

Page 57

A lovely dessert you can make by just putting castella, pudding, and whipped cream in a bowl and chilling.

★ ★

Ingredients:

2 small bananas

1 slice castella (see note on page 14 for castella substitutes)

1 store-bought flan (store-bought vanilla pudding cup may be substituted)

6¾ tablespoons whipping cream

1 teaspoon lemon juice

2 tablespoons sugar

2 tablespoons water

3 raisins

6 black sesame seeds

chocolate candy stick for decoration (optional)

Instructions: Makes 2 servings.

1. Mix 2 tablespoons of water and 1 tablespoon of sugar and microwave for 30 seconds. Once the mixture is cool, add 1 teaspoon of lemon juice to make the syrup.

2. Keeping the peel on, cut three ⅓-inch slices of the banana and sprinkle with lemon juice to prevent the banana from turning brown. Peel the rest of the banana and cut into 2-inch-round slices. Repeat with the other banana.

3. Add 1 tablespoon of sugar to the whipping cream and whip lightly.

4. Break apart half of the castella into two separate bowls. Pour the syrup over the castella.

5. Put half of the flan in each bowl over the castella. Then add the peeled bananas and then the whipped cream. Cover with plastic wrap and chill in the refrigerator.

6. Place the banana with peels on a plate and use a thinly sliced raisin and black sesame seeds to create the Combee faces.

7. Glue some paper that's been cut into a wing shape onto a toothpick and insert the toothpick into the banana.

8. Add a chocolate stick to the bowl of trifle if desired.

Tiny Bee Pokémon

Combee

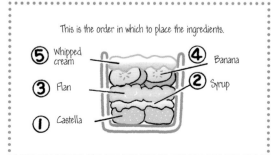

This is the order in which to place the ingredients.

⑤ Whipped cream
④ Banana
③ Flan
② Syrup
① Castella

Piplup Milk Gelatin

A white milk gelatin that uses jam to make Piplup's face. There are lots of peaches inside.

Page 56

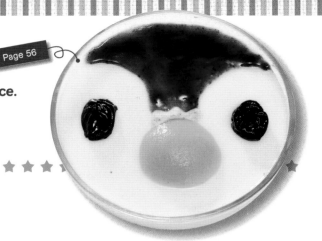

★ ★

Ingredients:

1¼ cups milk

3 tablespoons sugar

1 teaspoon gelatin

2 slices canned yellow peaches

1 prune

1 tablespoon blueberry jam (grape jam may be substituted)

¼ teaspoon vanilla extract (optional)

2 tablespoons water

Instructions: Makes 3 servings.

1. Soak the gelatin in 2 tablespoons of water.

2. Add the milk and sugar in a bowl and microwave for 2 minutes. Make sure to mix the sugar until it melts completely.

3. Add the gelatin to the bowl with the milk and sugar and mix well until the gelatin has melted. Add vanilla extract (optional).

4. Cut the round part of the peach and set aside for the bill. Cut the remainder into bite-sized pieces.

5. Place the cut peaches in a round bowl and add just enough gelatin mix to cover the peaches. Place in the refrigerator to chill.

6. Strain the blueberry jam. Take 1 tablespoon of the milk gelatin and add a little bit of the jam to make it light purple. Refrigerate.

7. When the gelatin in the bowl has hardened, carefully add the remaining gelatin mix and refrigerate.

8. Once all of the gelatin has hardened, top it with the two shades of blueberry jam, the prune pieces, and the peach nose to make Piplup's face.

Use the jam to create the forehead.

Cut the peach to proportionally match the size of the bowl.

Prune

Penguin Pokémon

Piplup

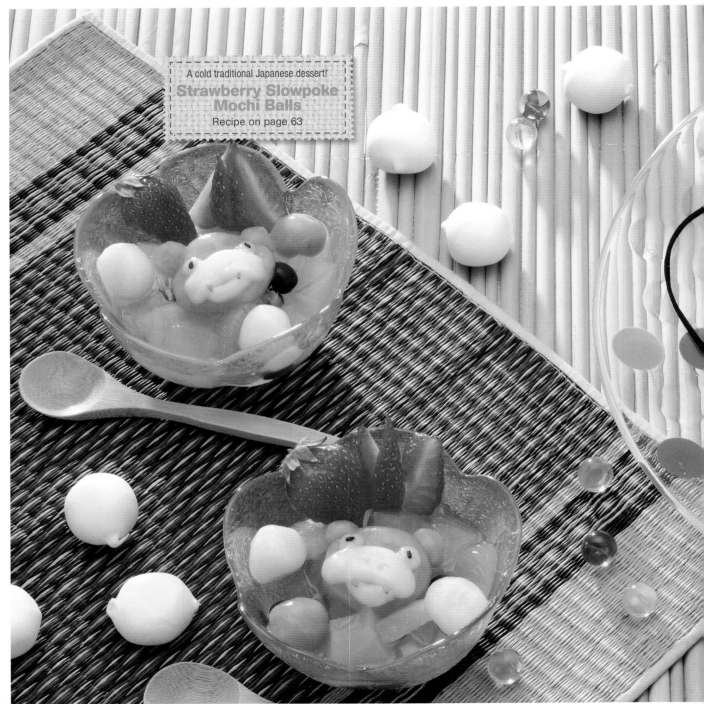

A cold traditional Japanese dessert!
Strawberry Slowpoke Mochi Balls
Recipe on page 63

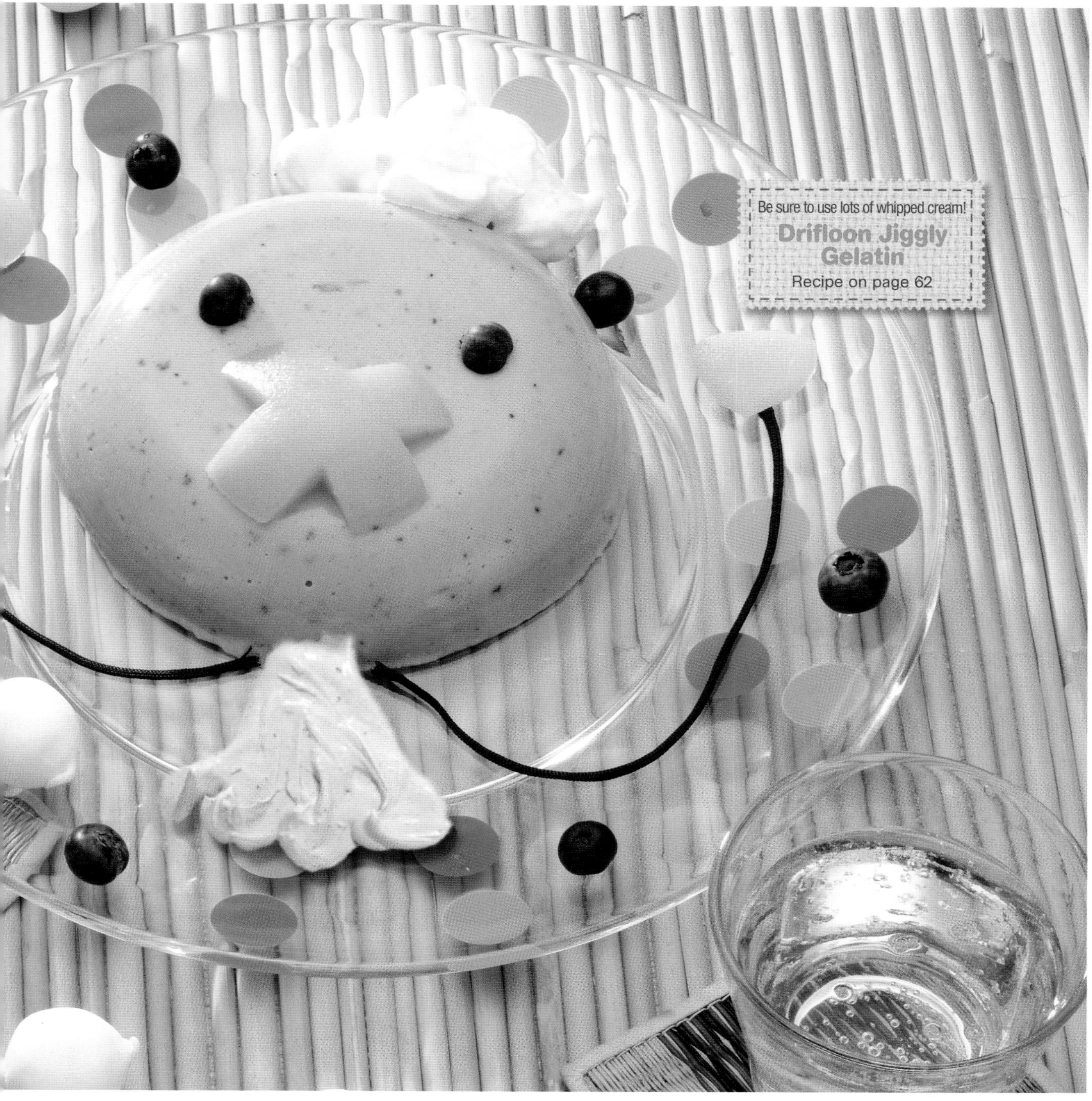

Be sure to use lots of whipped cream!

Drifloon Jiggly Gelatin

Recipe on page 62

Drifloon Jiggly Gelatin

A soft and creamy gelatin dessert that has lots of cream and yogurt. Make the arms from string or ribbon.

★ ★

Page 61

Ingredients:

½ cup + 2 tablespoons blueberry or grape jam

¾ cup plain yogurt

6½ tablespoons cream

1 teaspoon gelatin

5 tablespoons water

1 slice canned white peach

1 blueberry (2 raisins may be substituted)

3½ tablespoons sugar

Instructions: Makes 1 serving.

1. Soak the gelatin in 2 tablespoons of water.

2. Strain ½ cup blueberry jam into a bowl and mix with the yogurt, 3 tablespoons of sugar, and half of the cream.

3. Add 3 tablespoons of hot water to the gelatin to melt it and then mix it into the blueberry yogurt.

4. Chill the bowl in ice water and keep stirring until smooth.

5. Place it in a rounded bowl and refrigerate.

6. Place the bowl in some hot water for just a second to make it easier to remove the gelatin.

7. Add ½ tablespoon of sugar to the remaining cream and beat until fluffy. Place half on top of Drifloon's head. Mix the other half with 2 tablespoons blueberry jam to make the body.

8. Cut the peach to make the mouth and hands. Cut a blueberry in half to make the eyes.

Balloon Pokémon

Drifloon

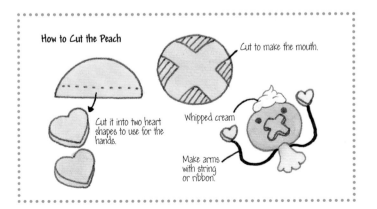

How to Cut the Peach

Cut to make the mouth.

Cut it into two heart shapes to use for the hands.

Whipped cream

Make arms with string or ribbon.

Slowpoke Strawberry Mochi Balls

Page 60

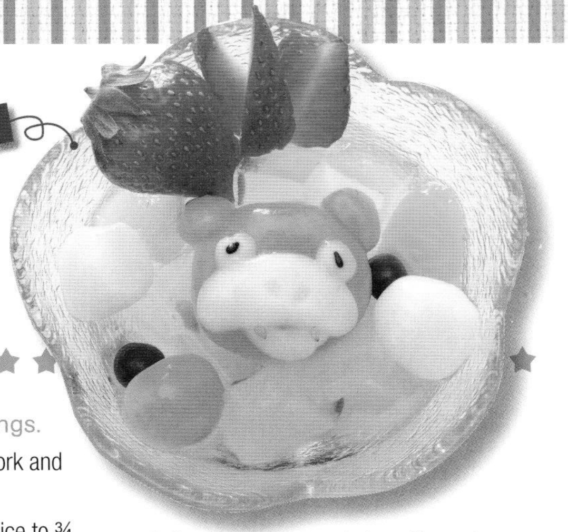

We made a Slowpoke by adding strawberry juice to white mochi balls.

Ingredients:

- 1½ ounces shiratama powder* (tapioca powder may be substituted)
- 4–5 strawberries**
- 2 white sesame seeds
- 2 black sesame seeds
- 1 can mitsumame*** (fruit cocktail may be substituted)
- ½ cup fruit of your choice

**Shiratama (white ball) is a mochi powder that you add water to and boil to make into a dessert. There's not much flavor to it, so it's always eaten with something else. It's similar to the tapioca balls found in boba/bubble tea.*

***If you can't get strawberries, use strawberry syrup that's used for shave ice.*

****Mitsumame (honey/syrup and red beans) is a traditional Japanese dessert that has red beans, gelatin cubes, and fruit—usually tangerines and peaches. It usually comes in a can. This may be substituted with a can of fruit cocktail.*

Instructions: Makes 2 servings.

1. Mash 1 or 2 strawberries with a fork and strain them for their juice.
2. Add 1 tablespoon of strawberry juice to ¾ ounces shiratama powder and knead until smooth.
3. Use half of the strawberry shiratama to create two Slowpoke. Ball up the remainder in a ½-inch ball.
4. Add 1 tablespoon of water to ¾ ounce of shiratama powder and knead. Make Slowpoke's mouth and eyes and ball up the rest. Make the eyes and fangs with sesame seeds.
5. Boil water in a pot and place Slowpoke and the mochi balls inside. Once they float to the surface, boil for an additional 2 minutes. Remove from the pot and place in cold water to chill.
6. Put the mitsumame and fruit into a bowl and place Slowpoke and the mochi balls on top.

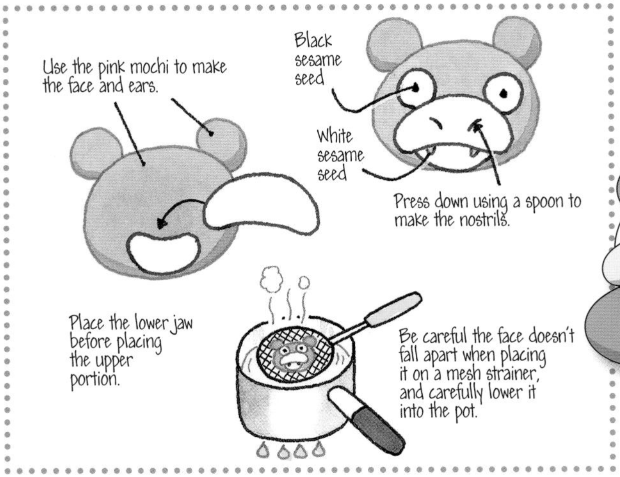
Use the pink mochi to make the face and ears.
Black sesame seed
White sesame seed
Press down using a spoon to make the nostrils.
Place the lower jaw before placing the upper portion.
Be careful the face doesn't fall apart when placing it on a mesh strainer, and carefully lower it into the pot.

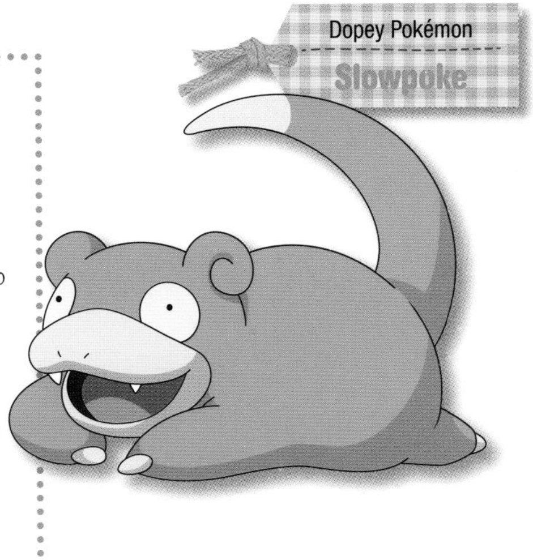
Dopey Pokémon
Slowpoke

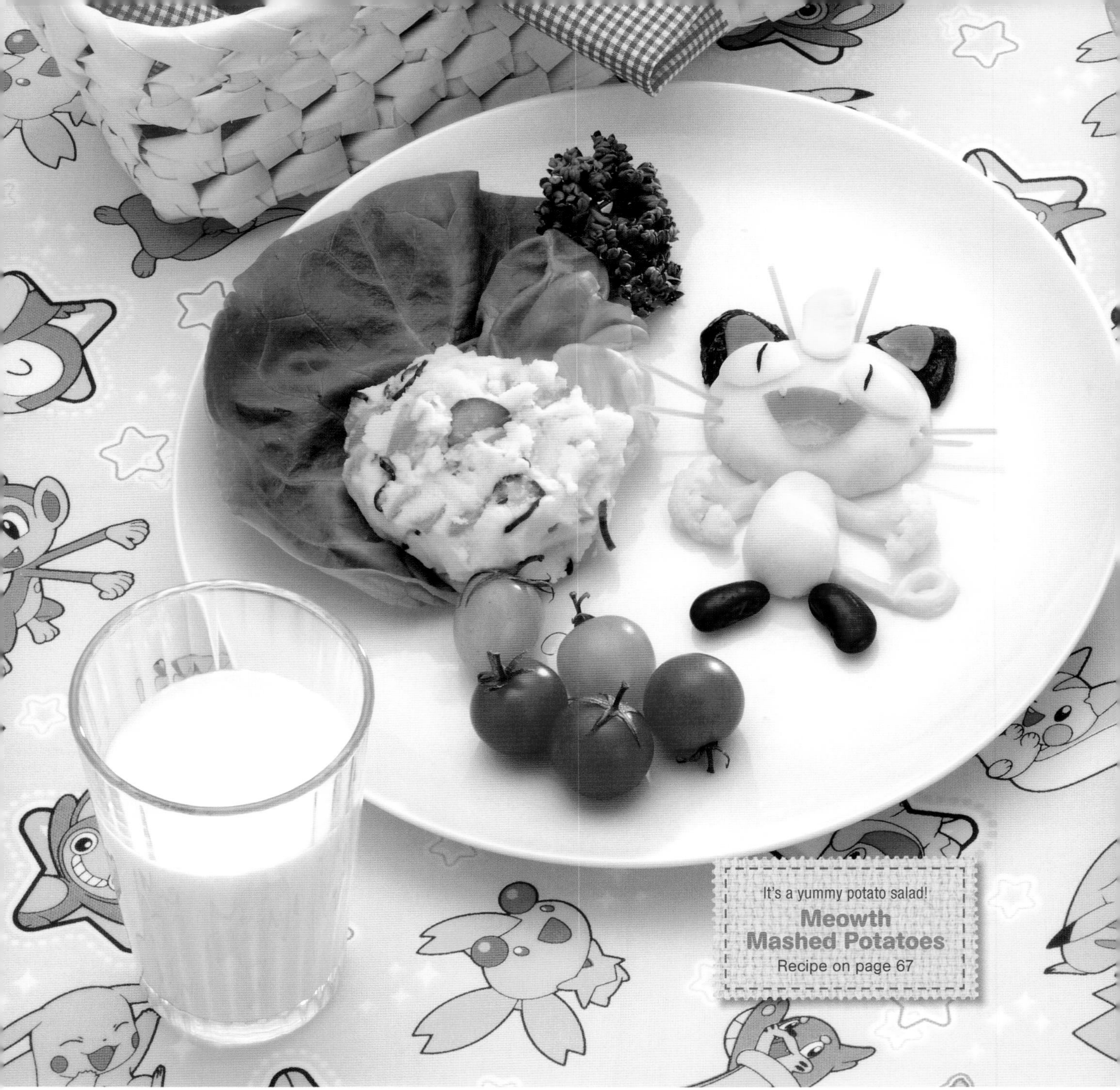
It's a yummy potato salad!
Meowth
Mashed Potatoes
Recipe on page 67

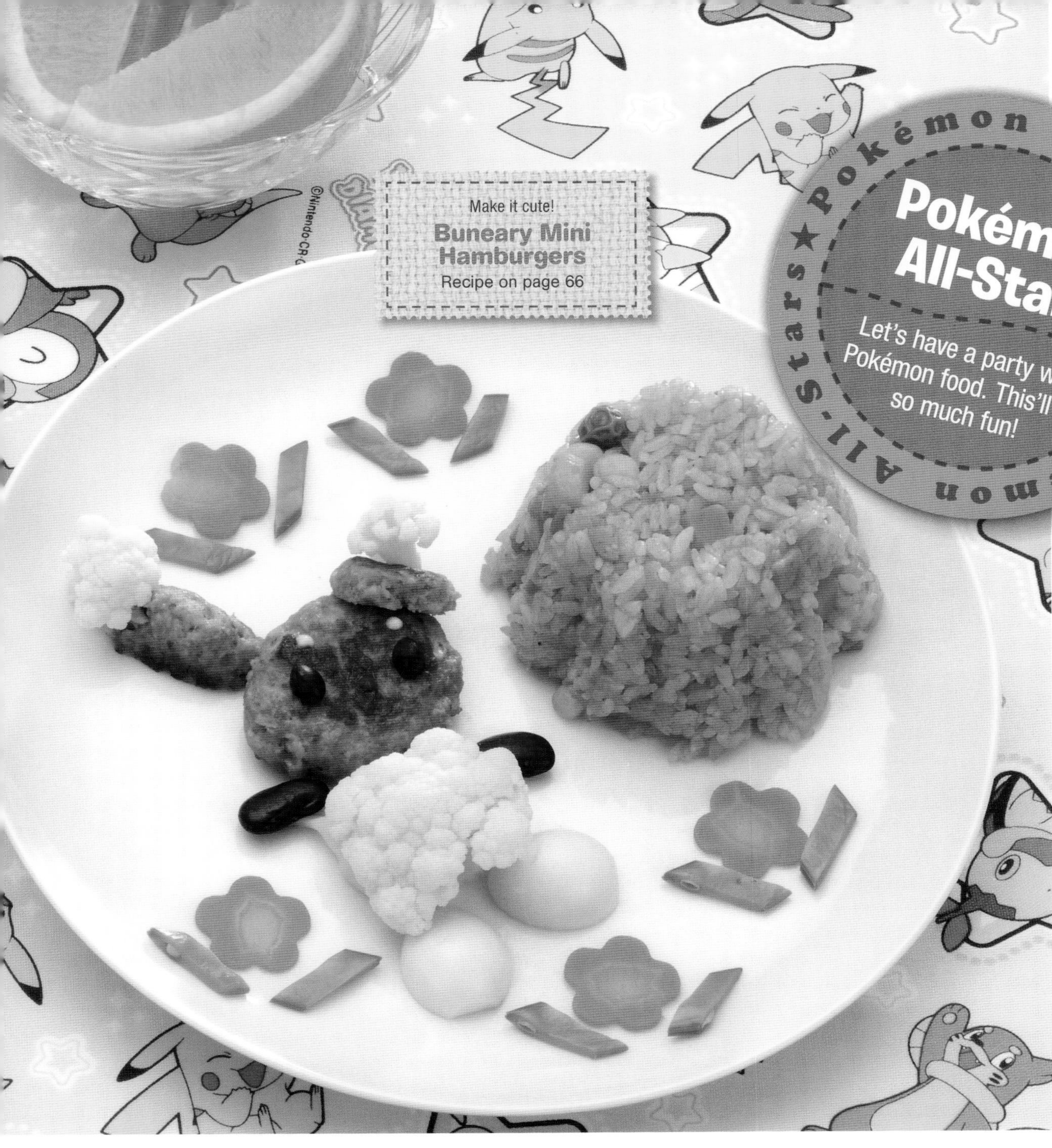

Make it cute!

Buneary Mini Hamburgers

Recipe on page 66

Pokémon All-Stars

Let's have a party with Pokémon food. This'll be so much fun!

Buneary Mini Hamburgers

Cauliflower is like white broccoli. We'll boil it here. Eat it with mayonnaise if you like.

★ ★

Page 65

Ingredients:

3 premade, store-bought small hamburger patties

2–3 florets cauliflower

2–3 red kidney beans

1 hard-boiled egg or quail egg

⅛ teaspoon mayonnaise

Instructions: Makes 3 servings.

1. Cut cauliflower into smaller pieces. Add the pieces to a pot of boiling water until the cauliflower is softened.

2. Microwave the hamburger according to the package instructions.

3. Place the hamburger on a plate to make the face. Cut one hamburger as shown in the illustration to make the ears.

4. Use the cauliflower, kidney beans, and egg to create Buneary.

5. Use mayonnaise to make the dots on its forehead.

Helpful Hint

When boiling cauliflower, if you add 1 tablespoon of vinegar to the water, the cauliflower will come out really white. Once it's softened, remove the cauliflower from the water—no need to cool it in cold water.

Rabbit Pokémon

Buneary

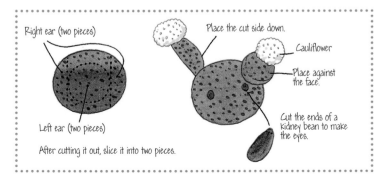

Right ear (two pieces)

Left ear (two pieces)

After cutting it out, slice it into two pieces.

Place the cut side down.

Cauliflower

Place against the face.

Cut the ends of a kidney bean to make the eyes.

Meowth Mashed Potatoes

If you've got mashed-potato mix, you don't need to use the stove top. Make the face with whatever you have in your kitchen.

Page 64

★ ★

Ingredients:

2 ounces mashed-potato mix

¼ cup milk

10 tablespoons warm water

2 tablespoons carrots

½ cucumber

2 tablespoons mayonnaise

1 teaspoon sugar

salt to taste

1 floret cauliflower

2 red kidney beans

1 prune

1 hard-boiled egg or quail egg

hijiki seaweed

1 cheese slice

sesame seeds

1–2 strands uncooked spaghetti noodle

Instructions: Makes 2 servings.

1. Cut the carrots into thin, round slices. Set aside 2 to 3 slices for the face, and cut the rest into quarters. Sprinkle a little salt over the carrots.

2. Boil one cauliflower floret in hot water and remove. Then boil the carrots.

3. Mix the mashed-potato mix with the milk and warm water. Set aside ¼ cup to make two Meowth. Mix the remainder with 2 tablespoons mayonnaise, 1 teaspoon sugar, and a little salt.

4. Squeeze out excess liquid from the cucumber and add it with the carrots to the mashed potato to make potato salad.

5. Make Meowth's head and body with the mashed potatoes that were set aside earlier. Put them on a plate.

6. Make Meowth's hands and feet with the cauliflower that's been cut into small pieces and the kidney beans.

7. Cut the prune in half and use that with the carrot to make the ears. Make the mouth with a carrot slice and add sesame seeds to make the fangs.

8. Make the gold coin from a cheese slice. Use small pieces of spaghetti to make the whiskers.

Scratch Cat Pokémon
Meowth

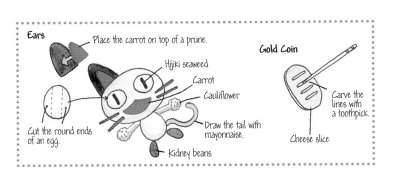

Ears — Place the carrot on top of a prune.

Hijiki seaweed

Carrot

Cauliflower

Draw the tail with mayonnaise.

Cut the round ends of an egg.

Kidney beans

Gold Coin

Carve the lines with a toothpick.

Cheese slice

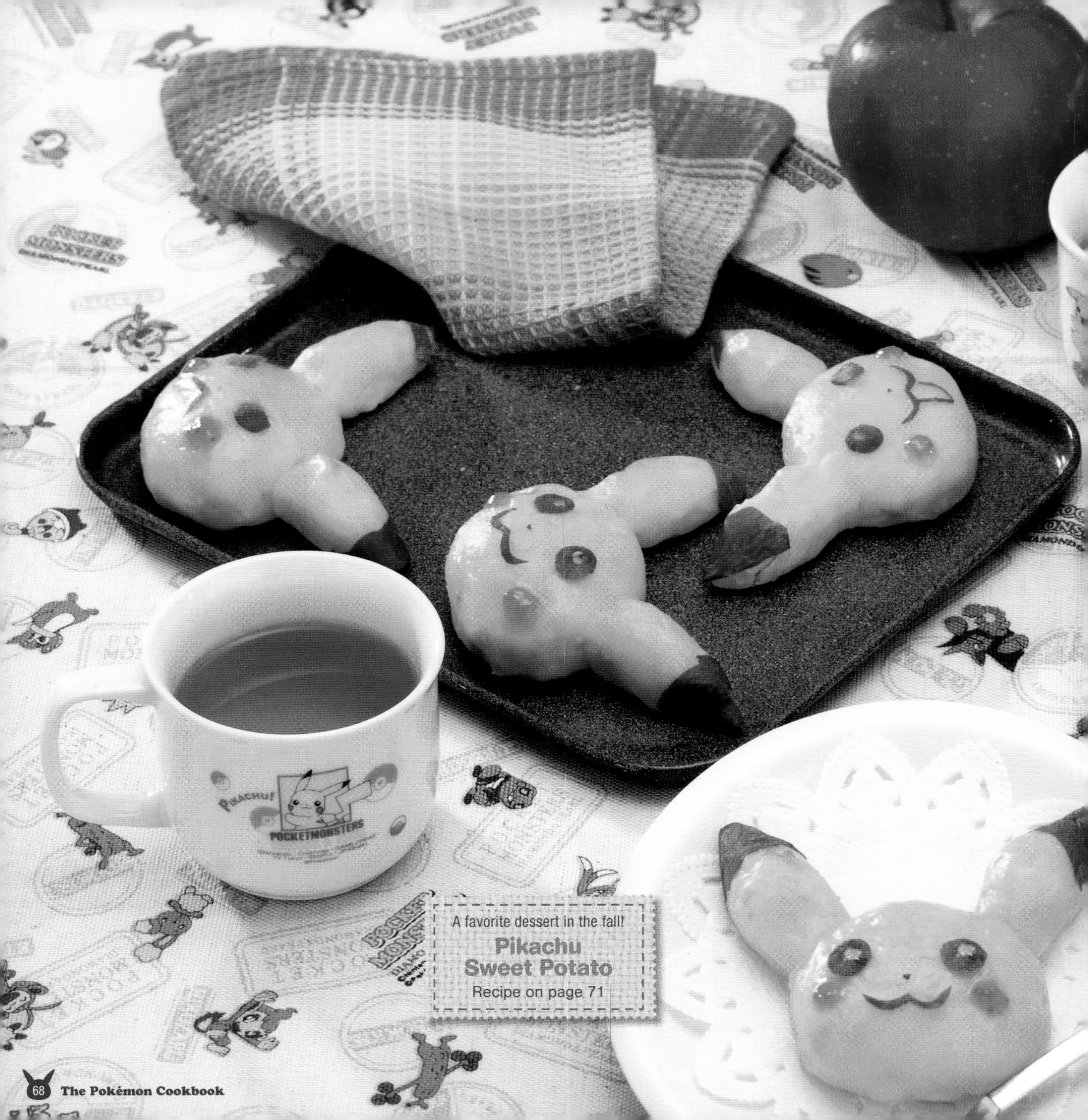
PIKACHU!
POCKETMONSTERS

A favorite dessert in the fall!

Pikachu Sweet Potato

Recipe on page 71

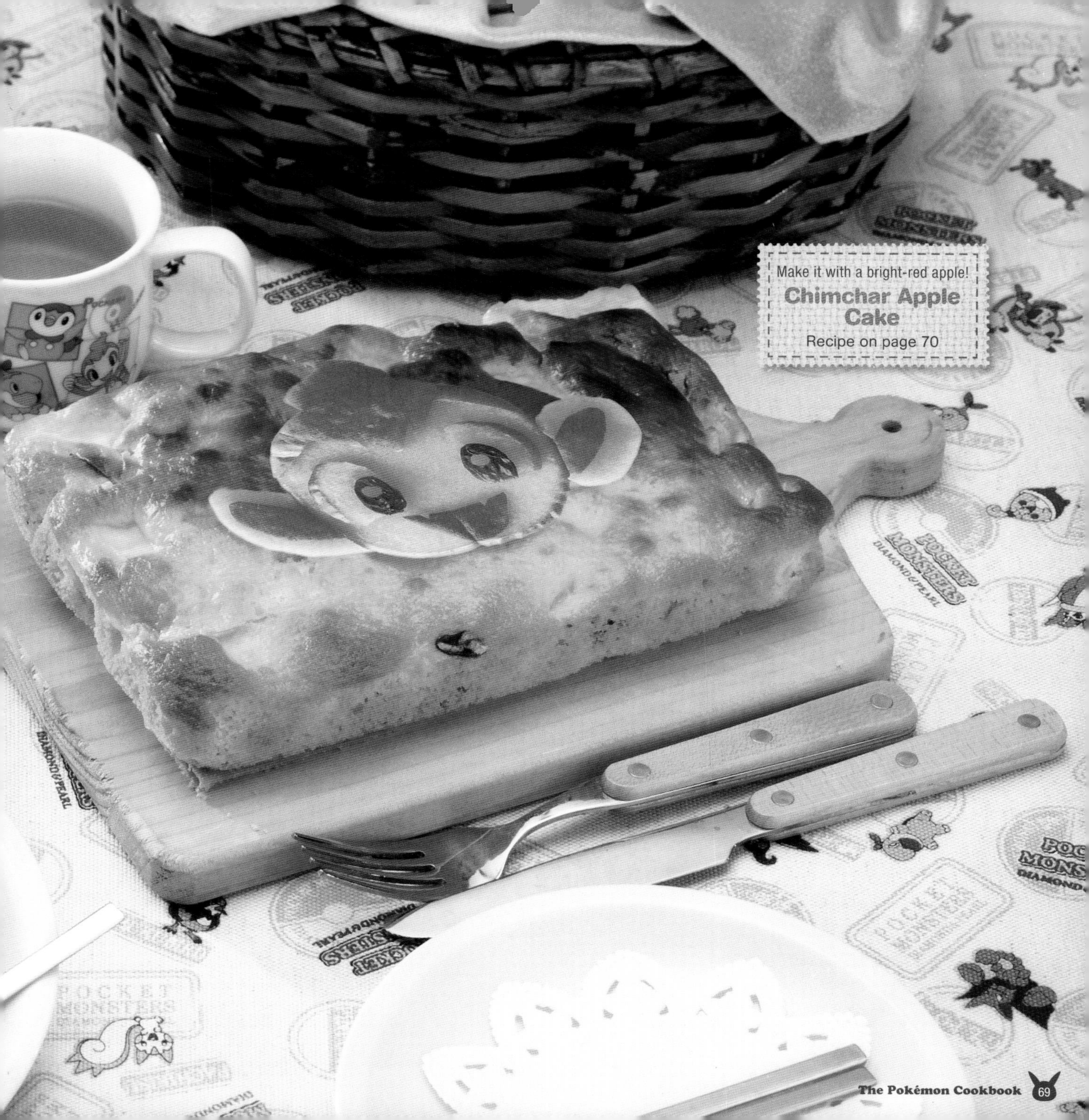
POCKET MONSTERS
DIAMOND&PEARL

Make it with a bright-red apple!

Chimchar Apple Cake

Recipe on page 70

Chimchar Apple Cake

A fruity cake that has a sweet apple baked into it. You'll make it with pancake mix.

Page 69

★ ★

Ingredients:

1 apple

¼ cup sugar

¾ cup pancake mix

1 egg

2 tablespoons milk

1 tablespoon vegetable oil

2 tablespoons raisins

Instructions: Makes 1 serving.

1. Place parchment paper inside a cake pan (11 inches by 7 inches). Set one raisin aside. Put the rest in warm water.

2. Slice the apple as shown in the illustration. Remove the core and cut the remaining pieces into quarter rounds.

3. Place the apples in a microwave-safe bowl and sprinkle 2 tablespoons of sugar on top. Let sit for 10 minutes and then microwave for 5 minutes. Set aside to cool.

4. Use scissors to cut the apple into Chimchar's face as shown in the illustration.

5. Make the cake batter: Mix the egg, the remaining sugar, and the milk in a bowl. Add the pancake mix and stir until smooth. Add the vegetable oil, the raisins, and the rest of the apple.

6. Pour the batter into the cake pan evenly. Cover with aluminum foil and bake in a toaster oven for 12 minutes or a conventional oven at 350°F for 25 to 30 minutes. When the cake rises, remove the foil and bake for an additional 3 minutes.

7. When the cake cools, remove from the pan and place Chimchar's face on top.

Chimp Pokémon

Chimchar

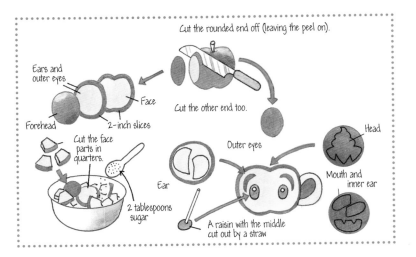

Cut the rounded end off (leaving the peel on).

Ears and outer eyes

Face

Cut the other end too.

Forehead

2-inch slices

Cut the face parts in quarters.

Outer eyes

Head

Ear

2 tablespoons sugar

Mouth and inner ear

A raisin with the middle cut out by a straw

Pikachu Sweet Potato

Page 68

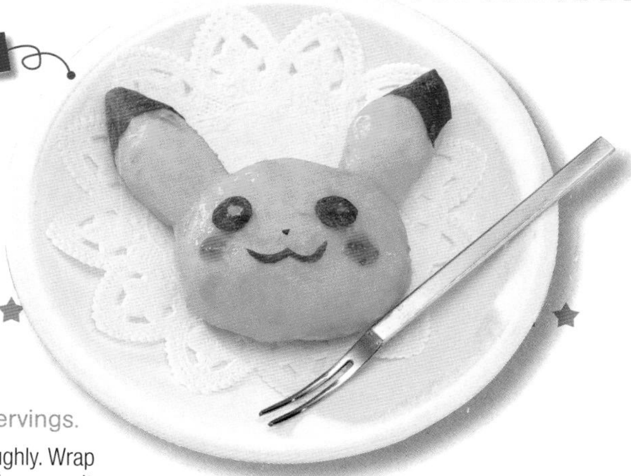

A baked sweet potato becomes a yummy treat. It pairs well with milk tea.

Ingredients:

- 1 medium-sized Japanese sweet potato (about 11 ounces)
- 3 tablespoons sugar
- 3 tablespoons butter
- 1 egg yolk
- 1 teaspoon strawberry jam

Helpful Hint

If the sweet potato is too hard to mash, use a pestle. If it's dry and crumbly, add some milk.

Instructions: Makes 4 servings.

1. Wash the sweet potato thoroughly. Wrap it in a wet paper towel and microwave it for 3 to 5 minutes, or until soft.
2. Once it's cool to the touch, remove it from the microwave and cut it into chunks. Remove the skin and set it aside.
3. Put the sweet potato in a bowl and mash it with a fork. Mix in the sugar and butter.
4. Whisk the egg yolk. Set aside ½ teaspoon of the yolk and mix the rest with the sweet potato.
5. Make four Pikachu heads with the sweet potato and place it on a toaster oven pan.
6. Mix the ½ teaspoon of egg yolk with a little water and brush it onto the Pikachu heads.
7. Cover the four Pikachu with aluminum foil and bake at 350°F for 5 to 10 minutes.
8. Make Pikachu's face with the potato skin and strawberry jam.

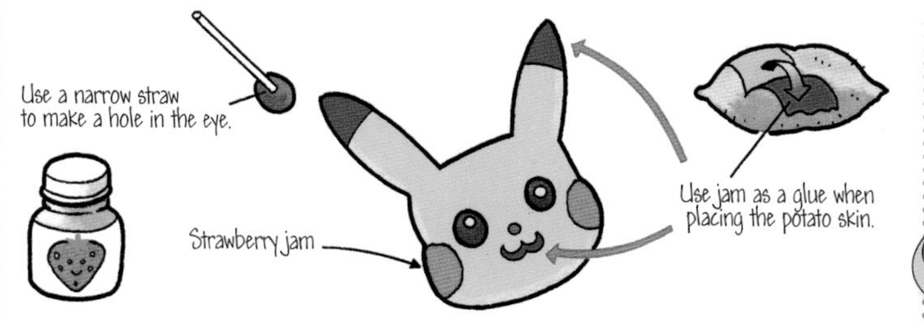
Use a narrow straw to make a hole in the eye.
Strawberry jam
Use jam as a glue when placing the potato skin.

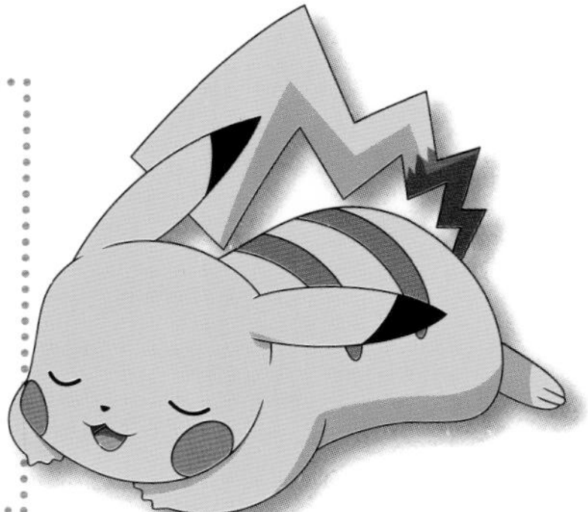

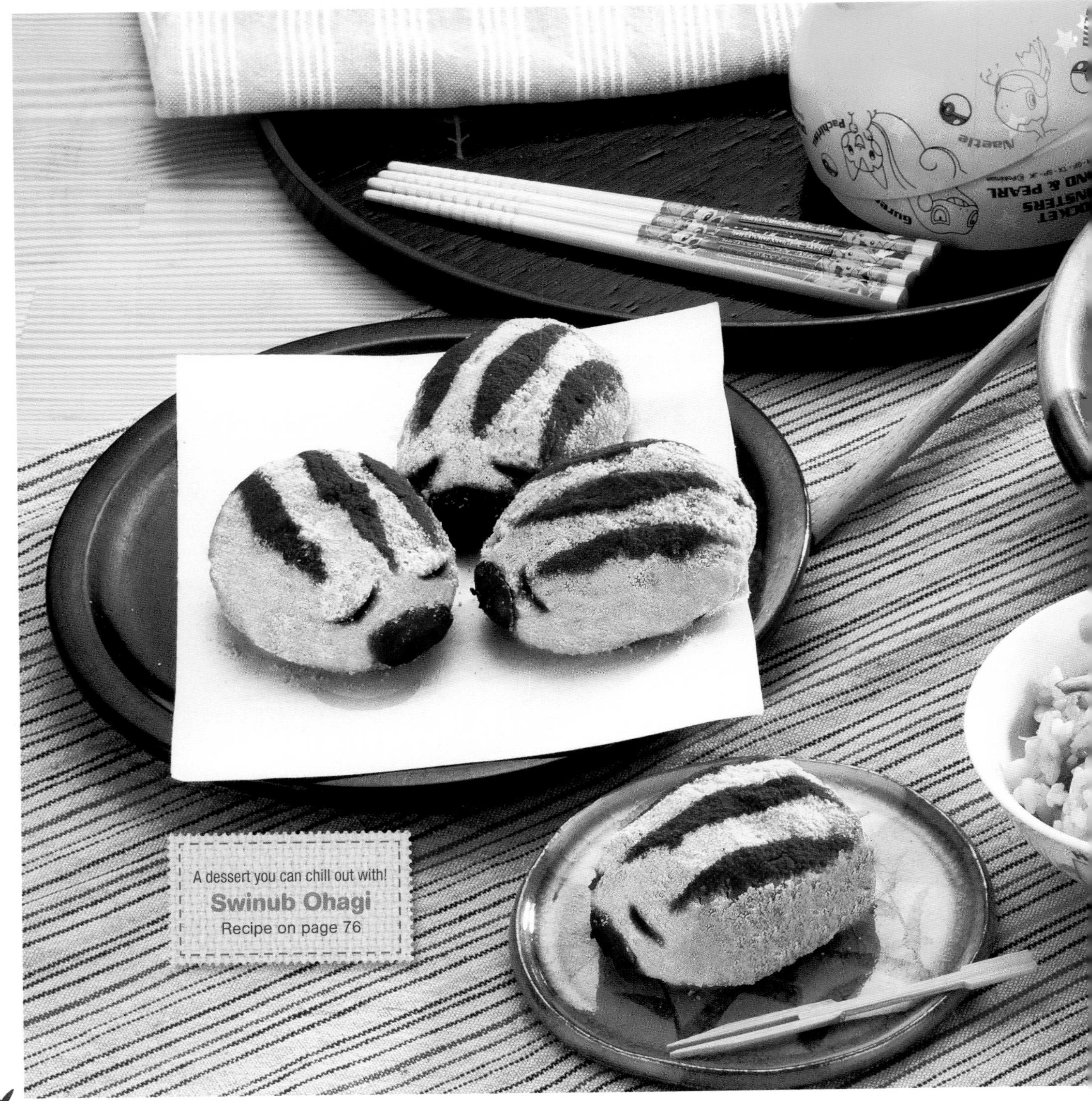

A dessert you can chill out with!

Swinub Ohagi

Recipe on page 76

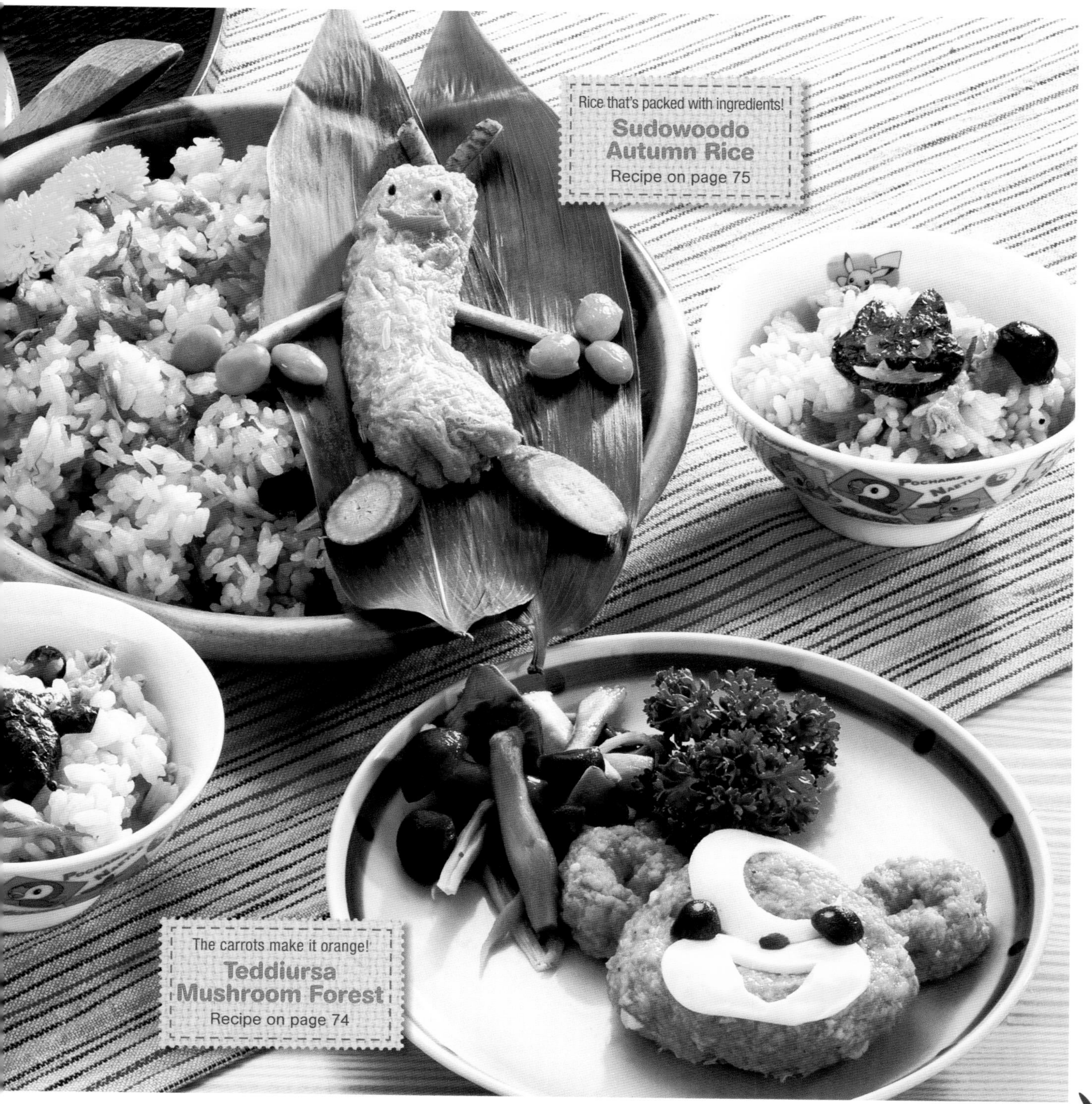
Rice that's packed with ingredients!
Sudowoodo Autumn Rice
Recipe on page 75
The carrots make it orange!
Teddiursa Mushroom Forest
Recipe on page 74

Teddiursa Mushroom Forest

You can make this chicken burger in the microwave. The carrots are mixed into the meat, so you won't even know they're there!

Page 73

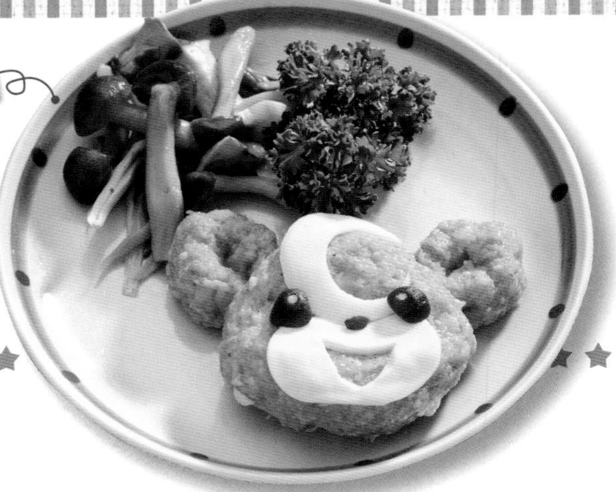

Ingredients:

- ¾ cup minced chicken
- ¼ cup carrots
- ⅛ cup panko bread crumbs
- ½ teaspoon salt
- pinch of pepper
- 1 slice kamaboko (fish cake), or substitute another slice of cheese
- 1–2 cheese slices
- ½ pack shimeji mushrooms
- ½ pack maitake mushrooms
- ½ pack king oyster mushrooms
- 1 tablespoon butter

Instructions: Makes 2 servings.

1. Grate the carrots and knead them with the minced chicken, the panko bread crumbs, the salt, and a little pepper.
2. Knead it until sticky. Cover it with plastic wrap and refrigerate for 1 hour.
3. Form two Teddiursa heads from the meat and microwave for 5 minutes.
4. Trim the bases off the shimeji, maitake, and king oyster mushrooms and separate them so they're easier to eat. Place in a bowl and microwave for 2 to 3 minutes.
5. Add butter to the mushrooms and stir.
6. Make Teddiursa's face with the kamaboko, cheese slice, and shimeji caps.
7. Place the mushrooms on the plate.

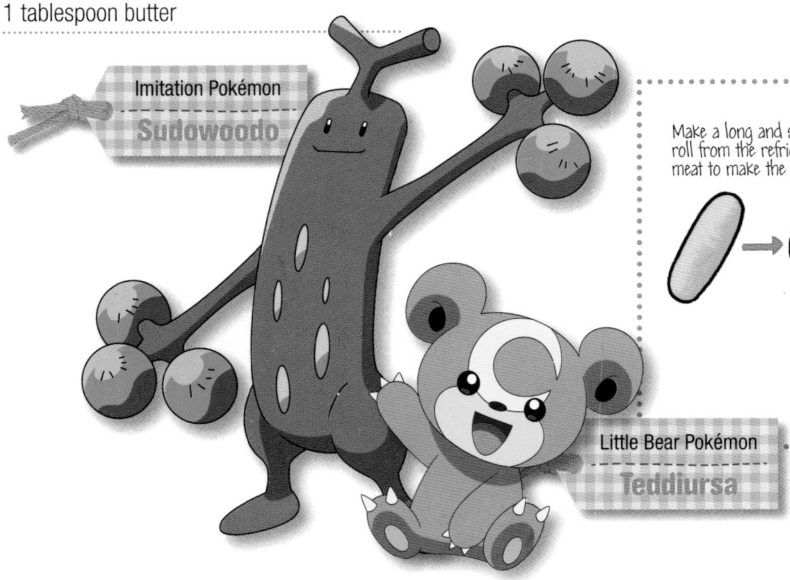
Imitation Pokémon
Sudowoodo
Little Bear Pokémon
Teddiursa

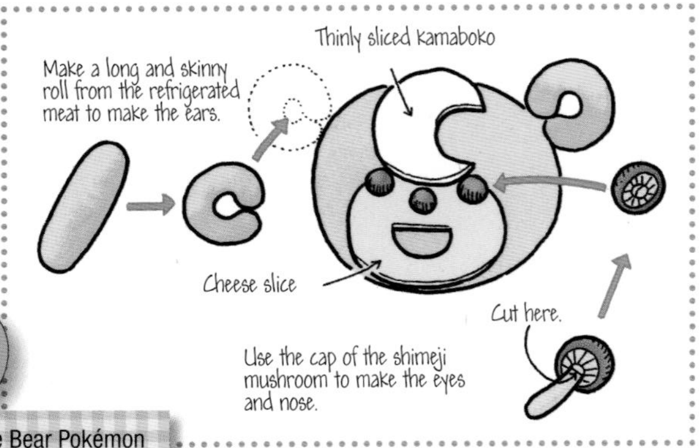
Make a long and skinny roll from the refrigerated meat to make the ears.
Thinly sliced kamaboko
Cheese slice
Cut here.
Use the cap of the shimeji mushroom to make the eyes and nose.

Sudowoodo Autumn Rice

Just add burdock root, mushrooms, and carrots to rice and cook in a rice cooker. Easy peasy!

Page 73

Ingredients:

- 2 cups uncooked rice
- ¼ cup burdock root
- 2 tablespoons carrots
- 1 aburaage / deep-fried tofu pouch
- ½ pack shimeji mushrooms
- ⅞ cup water
- 6 shelled edamame
- edible chrysanthemum, for decoration (optional)
- 2 black sesame seeds
- ¼ cup noodle soup concentrate

Instructions: Makes 4 servings.

1. Rinse the rice several times. Once finished, soak it in water.
2. Cut the burdock root and fried tofu as shown in the illustration. Julienne the carrots and remove the base of the shimeji mushrooms. Separate the mushrooms individually.
3. In a small pot, add the soup concentrate to ⅞ cup of water. Add the burdock root, fried tofu, carrots, and mushrooms and simmer on low heat. When it boils, let it simmer for 3 more minutes before turning off the heat.
4. When the soup base has cooled, place a colander over a bowl and separate the stock from the vegetables.
5. Put the drained rice in the rice cooker and add the stock. Add additional water to fill to the water line and cook.
6. Once the rice has cooked, add the vegetables (aside from the ones being used to create Sudowoodo) and mix.
7. Make a long rice ball and place it inside the tofu pouch to create Sudowoodo's body.
8. Complete Sudowoodo with the burdock root, edamame, edible chrysanthemum, black sesame seeds, and carrots. Place on top of the rice and you're done!

Aburaage / Fried Tofu
Burdock Root
Shimeji mushrooms
Julienned carrots
Black sesame seed
Carrot
Burdock root
¾ inch
Julienne the rest.
Cut diagonally (feet)
1½ inches
Thick julienne cuts (arms and horn)
Shred the rest.
Sudowoodo's body
Simmer the noodle soup base.
Make a long, skinny rice ball and insert it inside the tofu pouch.
Chrysanthemum petals
Edamame
Burdock root

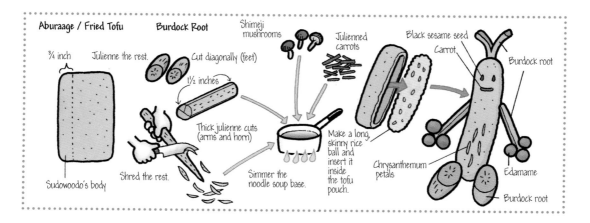

Swinub Ohagi

All you have to do is sprinkle cocoa powder on top of a kinako ohagi! Just be careful not to sprinkle too much cocoa or else it'll taste bitter.

Page 72

★ ★

Ingredients:

1 store-bought kinako ohagi,* or substitute cream-filled snack-sized cake

1 amanatto bean** (kintoki variety), or substitute chocolate candy disk or chocolate-covered raisin

½ cup cocoa powder

2 black sesame seeds

Instructions: Makes 1 serving.

1. Make the stripe patterns using a postcard-sized piece of paper. Put the cocoa powder in a strainer and sprinkle over the cutout paper that you place on top of the ohagi. These will be the stripes.

2. Remove the sugar from the amanatto bean and cut the bean in half. Place one piece on the nose area. The black sesame seeds will become the nostrils.

3. Wet the bottom tip of a small spoon and dip it into the cocoa powder. Draw the eyes by pressing the spoon into the ohagi where the eyes would be.

*Ohagi is a traditional Japanese dessert that is oblong in shape. It has mochi rice in the center and is covered by a red bean paste. For the kinako version, the red bean is in the center and is surrounded by the mochi rice. It is then covered with kinako powder (soybean powder).

**Amanatto are sweet boiled beans that have a sugar coating. There are different varieties of them—red beans, white beans, black beans, etc. Kintoki is the red kidney bean version.

Helpful Hint

For the cocoa, use either pure cocoa that has no sugar or milk added or cocoa powder that's used for baking.

Pig Pokémon
Swinub

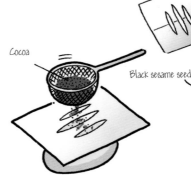

Fold the paper in half and cut out the pattern using scissors.

Cocoa

Black sesame seed

Remove the kinako powder where the nose would be and place the amanatto bean there.

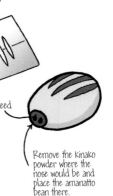

Cooking Technique Lesson 3

How to Create Characters Easily

Here are some tips for re-creating favorite Pokémon in your dishes. There may be some detailed work necessary, but you'll be satisfied when you see the outcome!

Look at the Example!

Once you've decided which recipe to make, take a look at the Pokémon carefully to figure out its characteristics. Note the eyes, the mouth, how the face is balanced, and the balance between its head and body!

Use Paper Patterns!

When making the parts for the Pokémon, don't just start to cut willy-nilly. First, make the pattern out of paper so you can figure out how big it should be! Once you see how it all balances out, you can cut the ingredients using the paper as a guide.

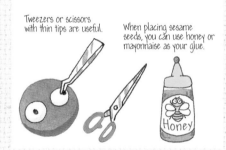

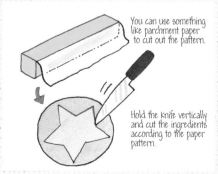

You can use something like parchment paper to cut out the pattern.
Hold the knife vertically and cut the ingredients according to the paper pattern.

About the Small Parts...

When cutting out the small parts, it'll be easier if you use a thin paring knife. Box cutters and tweezers are useful too. Be sure to disinfect them with alcohol before you use them though.

Tweezers or scissors with thin tips are useful.
When placing sesame seeds, you can use honey or mayonnaise as your glue.
Honey

Use What You Have!

You don't have to be exact when making them. If you have fun making them and they taste good, that's the important thing. Don't feel you have to stick to the tools and ingredients listed in this book. Use whatever you have already in your kitchen!

INDEX by Food Category

【Rice】

【Bread & Noodles】

【Meat & Vegetables】

【Desserts】

INDEX by Character

About the Author

Author and nutritionist Maki Kudo was born in Nagano Prefecture in 1961 and graduated from Seikei University's Literature Department in 1985. In 2002, she enrolled in the Food and Nutrition Department at Jissen Women's Junior College. She writes articles on cooking, nutrition and food education.

The Pokémon Cookbook Easy & Fun Recipes
by Maki Kudo

Original Japanese edition published by SHOGAKUKAN.
English translation rights in the United States of America, Canada, the United Kingdom, Ireland, Australia and New Zealand arranged with SHOGAKUKAN.

Illustrations/Katsumi IKEJIRI, Kazuya OGITA

English Adaptation/Elizabeth Kawasaki, pinkie-chan
Translation/pinkie-chan
Design/Izumi Evers
Senior Editorial Director/Elizabeth Kawasaki

Printed in China

Published by VIZ Media, LLC
P.O. Box 77010
San Francisco, CA 94107

10 9 8 7 6 5 4 3 2 1
First printing, December 2016

VIZ MEDIA
www.viz.com